SHERLOCK HOLMES

By the same author:

The British Hearse and the British Funeral, Book Guild Publishing, 2011
Sherlock Holmes: The Missing Earl and Other New Adventures, Book Guild Publishing, 2012

SHERLOCK HOLMES

*A Case at Christmas
and Other New Adventures*

*A selection of cases published by arrangement with
the estate of the late Doctor Watson, M.D.*

N.M. Scott

Book Guild Publishing
Sussex, England

First published in Great Britain in 2012 by
The Book Guild Ltd
Pavilion View
19 New Road
Brighton, BN1 1UF

Typesetting in Baskerville by
Keyboard Services, Luton, Bedfordshire

Printed in Great Britain by
CPI Antony Rowe

A catalogue record for this book is available from
The British Library

ISBN 978 1 84624 828 3

For friends and relatives in WA

Contents

1

The House on Holland Park

'Watson, Watson!' I was being shaken mercilessly out of a fitful slumber, Holmes leaning over the covers, shining a spirit lamp in my face. It was half past four in the morning.

The reason for the alarm: a night constable had apparently woken up Mrs Hudson, who in turn came upstairs and delivered an urgent message from Inspector Lestrade. For some reason, at this ungodly hour, we were expected to hasten to Kensal Green cemetery.

'Well, well', said Holmes as we rattled along in a hansom. 'Settle back my dear boy. I perceive by the wrought-iron clock above the pharmacy that it's five past five. The sun is rising over the rooftops of Marylebone and on this, the first day of spring, what could be more conducive to the spirit than an expedition to a north London cemetery, preceded of course by a trip along by the Union Canal and the gasworks? By Jove, let us count our blessings.'

Faint tendrils of smoke began to make an appearance from the bowl of his pipe as I myself filled my old briar with tobacco.

As dawn's early light suffused north London in

1

a fiery red glow, we arrived at Kensal Green cemetery. The constable on duty directed us to take the path that led from the easternmost entrance on Harrow Road. A number of officers of police were poking about amongst a conglomeration of granite sphinxes, marble angels and a turbaned Indian monument, with rakes.

Inspector Lestrade came across to greet us, his attempt to lighten the mood with cheerful banter falling somewhat flat. His hair was dishevelled, as were his clothes, and he had obviously not shaved.

He sighed wearily. 'Over here, if you please. Mind the masonry and the piled-up earth.'

'A grave was robbed,' said I, careful not to trip on the border of a plot covered by weeds. There was a coffin lid balanced against an obelisk. The grass thereabouts glistened with early morning dew. Holmes immediately took out his magnifying glass and studied the brass plaque, now green with age. I myself could make out the inscription:

Sir Hubert Coates
May He Rest in Peace

I was both shocked and horrified. It had taken the name of a famous historian and author to make me appreciate the seriousness of the crime: the wanton desecration of a grave belonging to one whose books were, even then, rightly judged as classics.

'My God,' said I, 'he's only been dead these past ten years. Do you mean to say the remains are missing?'

Lestrade merely nodded and puffed on his cigarette. I glanced across the mass of headstones and eccentric monuments, the sun now high in the sky above Kensal Green.

'Late last night, Todd, the night watchman, came across the opened grave.'

'A terrible business,' said I, leaning down and peering into the empty oak coffin tipped on its side, the taffeta lining mouldy and threadbare.

'Do either of you fancy breakfast? I haven't eaten for hours. There's a café at the Portobello Market, opens in about ten minutes,' asked the famished Scotland Yarder.

'I should fancy ham and eggs', said Holmes. 'But firstly, Inspector, tell me, did your men carry out a thorough search of the vicinity?'

'Indeed Mr Holmes. The Greek chapel, the catacombs, either side of the Central Avenue – all were meticulously searched.'

'Then might I draw your attention to a number of recent indentations upon the verge of the gravel drive used by hearses and mourning coaches?'

Lestrade coughed gruffly.

'Over here you will perceive a fresh footprint or two, but more importantly a clearly defined wheel rut. Thus our wagonette proceeds along the drive, the necessary dark lantern, pick and shovel, ropes and jemmies replaced on the conveyance at some stage. One of the wheels, however, not properly joined at the hub, tends to pitch the cart sideways.'

'I'll not argue the point, Mr Holmes.'

My companion set off along the avenue, coat tails flying, following the trail of the wagon with the crooked wheel, prodding the ground with his silver-topped cane.

At the cemetery gates, however, he spied a delivery cart identified by its sign as belonging to 'Topham's Dairy' lumbering up the road, and by now enlivened by a strong sense of purpose, directed the cart to pull over. The horse snorted, grateful for a rest from its labours.

The milkman was perched on the box seat holding the reins.

'I perceive your milk churns are empty. I see your round's finished, the deliveries done.'

'Indeed sir, two pats of full cream butter and a quart jug full of milk for Mrs Kelsey at No. 34. I'm for the yard now and then I'm back out again at nine.'

'Like us early morning ramblers, I trust you saw the sun rise over north London, a blaze of flaming colour?'

'But dreadful cold. We still have them frosts to contend with at this time of the year, don't we sir?'

'I'm wondering if perchance you might have met on your travels old Sedge from Camberwell doss house. The tramp treads these parts of a spring morning. Bound to be on the road.'

'No tramps did I see sir.' The milkman scratched his chin thoughtfully. 'But I did come across a gypsy caravan toddling along in the middle of the road. Not a care in the world have they, them tinkers sir.'

'Which way was the caravan travelling?'

'Along by the Union Canal, headed across the bridge towards Ladbroke Grove.'

'There's a coin or two in it for you if you can

share with me the exact spot you first encountered this carefree tinker.'

'Why, along the Harrow Road up by one of the gas lamps. Smoking a cigar he was. The gypsy told me he were travelling on to some horse fair.'

'How far down was it smoked?'

'What?'

'The cigar, halfway or a third?'

''Bout a couple of inches left I suppose.'

We bade the milkman good day and wished him well, watching his delivery cart trundle off down the road.

'Come Lestrade, my dear Watson,' said my friend, seizing my arm as we walked along, 'all of us for the time being must neglect our breakfast. We must instead painstakingly comb the pavements and verge along by the canal.'

'What on earth for?' said I.

'The rolled leaf butt of the tinker's smoked cigar of course. What a treasure. I myself can distinguish between one hundred and forty tobacco ashes. The opportunity of finding it offers a chance to identify at least one of the perpetrators responsible for defiling the grave. For I am convinced the gypsy caravan to which the milkman refers was but a subterfuge, a clever means of conveying the famous author's remains from the cemetery to an unknown location.'

We began checking the joins in between each paving slab, the kerbside clumps of weeds and grass along the road and after ten minutes or so of intensive searching Lestrade called out: he had found the rogue cigar butt perched precariously on the edge of a drain. A breath of wind could have sent it tumbling into the abyss of mouldy leaves and rainwater below.

Holmes snatched the cigar remnant and studied it with an expert eye. Spilling some tobacco ash into the palm of his hand he quickly reached a conclusion.

'Long Nines.' He threw the thing into the road and grimaced. 'A cheap cigar obtainable for a dime a basketful in the southern states of America, the Mississippi Delta. They are not for sale in Great Britain and indeed have thankfully never reached our shores for they are an acquired taste and would be abhorrent to the cultured English smoker.'

'Belonging to a person of poor means, an ex-cotton picker, a southern slave who worked on a tobacco plantation?' said I, putting forth my own view.

'Absurdly close Watson. However, I myself fancy that the Long Nines were imported at considerable cost by a person addicted to their strong, filthy flavour, from a young age. The class of that individual is hard to determine, but I should say he has money. Oh yes, a good deal of it. Come, I'm famished. All of us are in need of sustenance. Let us adjourn to the Portobello Market.'

That afternoon, the bright spring sunshine filled our sitting room and the familiar surroundings made a pleasant change from the north London cemetery, however imposing its funerary monuments or architecturally interesting the graves of its more famous incumbents.

My companion slung on his old threadbare dressing gown and leather slippers, slumped comfortably in his favourite armchair and smoked his long cherry wood pipe, staring with a weary, heavy-lidded expression out of the bow window at the roofs of the houses opposite, his brilliant mind delving into the case at hand, going over and over the tiniest morsel of evidence.

'Whoever would have thought it, my dear fellow, an American,' he murmured.

'Why, are they somehow exempt from committing crime?' said I, leafing through the newspaper.

'No, of course not. I simply meant to infer an American may be linked to the disappearance of the Sir Hubert Coates's remains.'

'Just consider the crime figures for Chicago, the Bronx, the Italian Quarter.'

'Watson!' said he, exasperated. 'Please be good enough to pass me that notepad and ink pen. Leave your insufferable crime figures to the statisticians. Now I shall attempt to compose an advertisement for inclusion in tomorrow's broadsheets.'

As the clock upon the mantelpiece ticked slowly, my friend deleted, added to and changed his composition for the umpteenth time, until, finally satisfied with the resulting script, he passed it over to me for approval.

I refilled my pipe with tobacco and found myself chuckling at his impertinence.

It read as follows:

Joseph Huxley and Professor Dunstan, antiquary and bibliophile respectively, are pleased to announce the sale of certain ephemera and memorabilia:

1 pair of pince-nez
1 fob watch chain
1 pair of breeches
1 mother's memoriam locket (gold)
1 foldable travelling desk

All the above property of the late Hubert Coates, esteemed author of *The Argonauts*, *Western Civilisation*, *Nile Quest*, etc. etc.

Interested parties need apply in writing to P.O. Box..., Baker Street.

'A pair of author's breeches.' I could barely contain my laughter. 'That is really going too far, Holmes. I think you shall receive a fairly modest postbag and let us hope no injunctions or writs from publishers or agents, nor the next of kin, but I see who you're aiming to ensnare. Obsessive collectors who will pay any amount of money to own some trinket once the property of a famous personality, whether it be authors or top-class cricketers.'

'Precisely, you have it exactly my dear fellow. Pray tell me, who would go to the bother of digging up one of the greatest authors who ever appeared in print, and who in his lifetime, and perchance in death, achieved a certain immortality?'

By the middle of the week, upon hearing of the terrible raid at Kensal Green cemetery, the nation was in a state of profound shock. Responding to public outrage, the Prime Minister had gone on record as telling the House, 'Never in our country's long and illustrious history has there been such a heinous act perpetrated against common decency and the world of literature. I abhor these despicable villains and I can assure the House each and every individual who took part in the dark deeds at Kensal Green shall be hunted down and eventually brought to justice.'

Meanwhile, we had received a few letters of interest concerning our advertisement placed in the daily papers. One was from a book dealer in Charing Cross, another from an elderly cleric who contacted us regarding the foldable desk and a third correspondent offering an astounding proposition.

The Ivy League Society of North America

Houghton Library
Harvard University

Yale University Connecticut

Rare Books and Manuscripts Library
Princetown University
New Jersey

Dear Mr Huxley and Professor Dunstan, we should be interested to consider your items re. H. Coates with a view to purchasing the same at favourable prices. Discretion assured. Provenance essential. I suggest we meet at nine of the clock tomorrow morning at my home.

London Agent
Shelby Jackson
10 Holland Park

This address, it turned out, was a fine Jacobean mansion opposite a densely wooded park from whence the exclusive, well-monied area not far from Kensington gets its name. We were met at the top of the steps of the impressive residence by an enormous and muscular black man, over six foot four in height, built like a heavyweight boxer, wearing an impeccably creased valet's uniform and white gloves. He gently guided us into the palatial hallway to be introduced to his master, Shelby Jackson.

'Welcome to my house gentlemen. Please come in and make yourselves comfortable. Deuteronomy Hoskins, a pot of tea for our guests. We'll take it in the drawing room.'

'Of course, sir,' the servant bowed and discreetly left us, closing the door behind him.

'Mr Huxley, the antiquary, Professor Dunstan, the bibliophile, I am delighted to make your acquaintance. Take a seat, gentlemen. Your advertisement in the daily news affected me most profoundly. I have these last eight years or so attended many auction room sales, private disposals of ephemera and letters, and have yet to encounter the elusive collapsible desk once belonging to Coates, upon which he wrote and composed those unforgettable classics of English literature – *The Argonauts, Western Civilisation* and *Nile Quest.* I and the clients I represent are ecstatic that this rare and valuable item has at long last surfaced on the open market. The memoriam locket is of special interest also.'

'My dear Mr Jackson,' said my colleague, taking on the role of the professor, an acclaimed bibliophile, 'you will appreciate that value and sentimental worth alas prevent us on this occasion allowing you to view the artefacts, but I can assure you that once I and Mr Huxley are convinced of your client's genuine commitment to purchase the collapsible travelling desk, memoriam locket and so forth, we shall lose no time in providing both provenance and a chance for you to minutely examine each article and make a final decision.'

During our conversation, I had ample leisure to study the Ivy League University's American representative, Shelby Jackson. Although short of stature I imagined when stripped he was swarthy as a gypsy. He was remarkably broad of the chest with large hips and spidery legs, wearing his frock coat and striped city trousers and buckled slippers he appeared every inch the southern gentleman, refined, worldly, obviously successful in business and well monied, making his fortune I surmised from tobacco or cotton. His impeccable manners and mesmerising charm left me in little doubt he was capable of anything good or evil to further his own ambition.

The door to the drawing room opened and in came Deuteronomy Hoskins. Proud to serve his master, the valet appeared with the tea things. I imagined those great unwieldy hands could crush a vertebrae with ease, break rocks from dawn till dusk in some prison chain gang, and yet his refined manners as he offered us each a cup and saucer from an exquisite bone china tea service was impressive. We chatted amiably for half an hour or so. At length we got up to leave.

'Your credentials are above reproach,' said I, taking up my top hat and stout ash stick. 'I believe a deal can be concluded swiftly. Would tomorrow at noon suit? Professor Dunstan and myself will bring the necessary papers and the Coates memorabilia. Anything to add, Professor?'

'Er, no, Mr Huxley', said Holmes in earnest.

'Let us shake hands on it.' Shelby Jackson gripped my hand in his and I was aware of a menacing gleam in his eye, an undercurrent of loathing, an understanding that in the natural order of things I was but a lesser mortal than he, a man without political influence, power and wealth. His hand was cold and clammy, his broad brow coated by a fine sheen of moisture.

Deuteronomy Hoskins grinned and showed us out, politely closing the front door behind us.

We returned later that night to Holland Park, Holmes with a set of assorted lock picks contained in a leather case, myself with the service revolver that had served us so well in the past. Our primary aim was to break into the impressive Jacobean mansion and lose no time making a thorough search of the premises in a desperate hope of discovering the whereabouts of the remains of Sir Hubert. Admittedly, neither of us could put hand on heart and say for sure Shelby Jackson was the organising force behind the desecration, but there was no doubting the American universities which he represented, Princetown, Harvard and Yale, had expressed a keen interest in Coates memorabilia. And what if their overriding requirements for assorted ephemera, letters, manuscripts and so forth extended to the dead author himself? I shuddered to think of the immense power brokered, the amount of funds available to these university libraries under the umbrella of the Ivy League.

Once Holmes had unlocked the front door, which luckily was not chained or bolted, we crept along the darkened hallway, my bull's-eye lamp shining on a mahogany chest, a set of etchings depicting plantation houses, a richly textured painting in oils. Unexpectedly the steel cap of my military boot thudded against the edge of a wooden packing crate. I nearly suffered a seizure for I was certain the noise would alert the occupants of the house. I saw Holmes was leaning flat against the wall like a limpet, praying we had not been found out. As our eyes became accustomed to the gloom, with mounting anxiety I had a growing sense we were being watched.

The lights came on, dazzling us. The noise I had chosen to ignore on the landing above, the muffled slow tread of slippered feet, now manifested in the form of the short and demonstrative Shelby Jackson. Deuteronomy Hoskins, wearing a set of striped pyjamas, was not far behind.

He lost no time in searching my pockets, quickly discovering my service revolver. With a look of utter disdain he slung it up the staircase and out of reach. Likewise Holmes was carefully searched.

The valet nodded to his master. 'Clear, boss.'

'Swell! So our friendly bibliophile and antiquary are returned. This time they choose to break into my property and arrive unannounced. You wish to steal my extensive collection of authors' ephemera and letters, I take it.'

'This is not what it seems,' said I, placing my lamp on top of the packing crate. 'We are totally innocent of any wrongdoing, our motives pure.'

'However,' said my companion, frowning intently, 'might I raise an objection concerning the illegal shipment of a corpse? That is presumably, Mr Jackson, what this crate contains.'

'You've overstepped the mark, sir. Deuteronomy, be good enough to show these gentleman into my study. We can talk better in there. I also keep my pistols handy inside my desk.'

I was nudged in the back by the hefty valet and shoved along the hall. Holmes was likewise manhandled. The fellow was far too fit and well built to take on. I knew he was gently simmering and if pressed might turn very nasty.

'You smoke Long Nines, Mr Jackson,' said Holmes, fingering a crumpled butt stubbed out in a crystal glass ashtray, one of a number of spent cigars. The atmosphere in the study reeked of foul, cheap tobacco. 'A habit no doubt picked up when you were but a callow youth, down south, Mississippi way. The brand is unique to the Delta. A dime a basketful. Alas, unfortunately for you and Deuteronomy here, I am a recognised expert on tobacco ash. I have even written a well-received monograph upon the subject. I think I have a trump card in my possession, Shelby.'

'What if you do?' He opened a drawer and retrieved a silver pistol. Considering the barrel, he checked each chamber. 'I choose to smoke a cheap brand of cigar, a dime a basketful, because I own the factories that make 'em. Should I be barred from your Reform and Athenaeum Clubs, not permitted to walk along Piccadilly of a fine spring morning to Burlington Arcade?'

'Not at all, you misunderstand me. The Long Nines irrevocably link you to the Kensal Green cemetery outrage, the gypsy caravan which you commandeered I am sure will not be too hard to trace. The caravan tended to veer to the left on account of a wobbly wheel not properly bolted to the hub. What a sight it must have been, you trotting along Ladbroke Grove in the early hours as dawn's opalescent light spread across the city. The remains of Sir Hubert Coates, one the most revered and famous authors in the country, wrapped in sacking, being watched over by Deuteronomy in the back. For who amongst us would suspect that a gaily painted caravan with a stove pipe chimney was in fact a hearse? That said I am going to ask you a fairly straightforward question, Mr Jackson – why?'

The southern gentleman, the agent for the Ivy League, took out his silk kerchief and dabbed his forehead. He appeared pale and agitated. He chose to be direct and truthful.

'It is our heritage, our right. The great historian and author Sir Hubert Coates belongs to us now. Coates shall be immortalised, held up to still greater glory. What does your nation care? It leaves its literary giants to moulder in neglected plots of weeds, untended and long forgotten. Think of the great pyramids, the pharaohs.'

'It's our heritage', said I. 'Sir Hubert was once a living, breathing author. It was his wish to be buried in a north London cemetery. What right have you to disinter him?'

15

'Tut, tut, you're petty English ways demean you, sir. The Ivy League has a grand plan. Consider the wider picture, gentlemen. Put your facile reasoning to one side.'

'What grand plan is this?' asked Holmes irritably, folding his arms, keeping his attention always fixed on Jackson's pistol. 'What great scheme have you in mind, I am emboldened to ask.'

'A wondrous, truly awesome mausoleum, an engineering accomplishment that the whole world shall marvel at. Nothing like it has been seen since the pharaohs, no expense shall be spared. A mausoleum constructed beneath the vast library of Harvard where is stored the world's finest collection of literary manuscripts, letters and ephemera, the author's remains displayed in a clear glass coffin upon a raised plinth of Carrera marble, a lecture theatre, a viewing room.'

'Yes, I think we catch your drift,' said I, wondering at the sheer determination of Shelby Jackson and how many more madmen there were like him, spurring him on in America, prepared to invest a fortune in the completion of such a vast subterranean 'folly'. Those of influence at Yale, Harvard and Princetown had much to answer for.

'A toast,' said Jackson, evidently bursting with new-found enthusiasm, grinning at his valet. 'The finest southern whiskey, a half measure each, straight from the "old Yankee cask" I keep down in my wine cellar for special occasions. We shall drink a toast to the Ivy League and good health to the proposed plan.'

'Sure thing, Mr Jackson, be a real pleasure. You

gen'lemen just wait here awhile. I'll fetch them pretty crystal glasses too.'

Sure to his word, the impressive southern valet swanned back into the room bearing a tray of drinks, a superb malt, the glasses temptingly half full of golden ambrosia. I was about to sample the whiskey, well matured in the cask, which I expected would have a strong woody flavour, when Holmes stayed my hand.

'Apologies. I have an allergy to 90 per cent proof "old Yankee firewater".'

Holmes brought his cane crashing down on Deuteronomy Hoskins's exposed wrist, cracking the bone with a loud snap. He yelled in pain, nursing the broken bone, the vast, powerful hand now limp and useless, the digits already swelling to the size of turkey drums. Meanwhile, I charged across the room and forcibly sent Shelby Jackson toppling over his desk. The silver pistol he held went flying across the room in the ensuing clumsy struggle. Jackson was a devil to contain. I wrapped my arms around his neck and tried to keep him from getting up.

It was only when my colleague thrust the gun barrel of the silver Colt revolver to his head and kept it cocked that the American became suddenly quiet and more amenable.

'You are both of you capable of cold-blooded murder,' said Holmes. 'That packing crate in the hall is worth killing for, yet how much more is it worth to the Harvard University Library, I wonder? I should not have fancied sampling your tainted whiskey, Shelby, becoming incoherent and drowsy before being shot in the back of the head, both of us weighted with lead and dumped in the canal.

'The packing crate will alas not be travelling on the White Star Line from Southampton across the Atlantic to New York. However, Mr Jackson, you and your valet most certainly will. I realise that even if I were to detain you and the police became involved, I am certain the American Consulate would intervene, employing a host of the finest lawyers on your behalf, such is the influence of the Ivy League Universities with their long association with past presidents, politicians and persons of wealth and influence. I doubt whether you would be detained for very long at her Majesty's pleasure. Our government would not risk our two great nations becoming embroiled in an international scandal. Get out of here, catch the train to Southampton. Be on your way, I say. For the alternative is that I and Doctor Watson may take the law into our own hands and deal with you far more severely. Do I make myself plain?'

'You are a true gentleman, sir. I appreciate your clemency. But tell me, why is your thinking so facile? Cannot you visualise the greater picture? Your worthy author to be further recognised, his reputation enhanced, for the planned subterranean mausoleum would attract countless visitors from all over the globe, keep his illustrious name forever in the public's memory.'

'Alas, your "Circus for the Dead" holds little fascination for me. The author shall be returned to his own plot at Kensal Green and there's an end to it.'

2

A Case at Christmas

The winter of 1892 was severe, the prolonged cold spell extending from the middle of December well into early March, and at its zenith causing untold chaos and misery to the populace of southern England. A dense pall of freezing Siberian air hung persistently over the capital.

One morning in late December I had every reason to curse Mother Russia for upon my return to 221b, I was covered from head to toe in gusting snow. Entering the hallway I stamped my feet once or twice on the mat to shake the worst of it off, then I made my way upstairs to our first-floor landing whence, in need of a welcome blast of fire, I proceeded to give my hat and coat a thorough and vigorous brush before entering our rooms. The door, I recall, was partly ajar and from within I could hear animated conversation taking place. There was a thick fug of tobacco smoke lingering in the air.

'Beethoven.' The old fellow grimaced. He was about one and sixty with grizzled side whiskers and grey silky hair. He was possessed of a bright, intelligent face and wore gold spectacles. His eyes were alive with good humour and friendly intent. 'Now I am not so keen on those big brash bombastic symphonies, Mr Holmes, all thunder and lightning.'

'Then might I suggest you try his adorable piano sonatas, Opus 14, 23 and 91 in particular,' suggested my companion, refilling his pipe with shag tobacco. 'I can assure you, you shall appreciate his symphonies better for listening to the sheer variety and tonal quality of his sonatas, else the more pushy piano concertos Nos. 1 and 2 stand up well. I am myself a late convert to Beethoven, Mr Franzen. Another whiskey?'

'Why, that's very generous of you I'm sure', said the old gentleman, much impressed by my colleague's evident grasp of classical music. 'And the Mendelssohn violin concerto?'

'*J'adore Mendelssohn, c'est magnifique, tres bien.*'

'Perfectly put Mr Holmes, perfectly put, ha ha.'

'Ah, my dear Watson, warm yourself by the fire. Might I introduce Mr Frederick Franzen of the Clock House in Kent. He has interrupted his schedule of teaching at a preparatory school in Dulwich to brave the foul wintry weather and unheated trains to present me with a most puzzling sequence of events in which he claims the Stradivarius Messiah violin was stolen.'

'The Messiah,' said I, lighting a cigar and gratefully accepting a proffered glass of whiskey. 'That is one of the rarest violins in existence – priceless beyond compare. An imitation you refer to, surely.'

'Alas, sir, I refer to the genuine article.' Franzen appeared mortified, a perplexed expression surfacing on his noble features. 'I should explain, Doctor

Watson, I am a music master. I have a pupil by the name of Broadhurst, who has been playing violin since the age of four and is what musicologists refer to as a prodigy of rare talent. My fault, I hold my hands up, but I could not resist allowing for our annual Christmas concert the little fellow a chance to play an instrument more worthy of his unique gift.'

'But how on earth did you come by the Messiah? It is surely kept under lock and key at the...'

'Ashmolean Museum, Oxford. Oh I know the place intimately. Not only was I an undergraduate at Oxford, but my younger brother Edward is presently curator of that hallowed establishment. It is thanks to him alone I owe the favour of a loan of the Stradivarius for one week only.'

'A week?' Holmes was unable to contain his amusement any longer. 'A week, why not a month?' He tamped down the strands of tobacco in the bowl of his pipe.

'A week in which the preparatory school Christmas concert was a success, a week in which young Broadhurst excelled playing Scarlatti and was feted thereafter by parents, pupils and teachers alike, a week in which I and my brother now find ourselves on the brink of disaster, infamy and ruin. I rest my case, gentlemen.'

'Very well,' said I. 'Before we continue I am intrigued to know, what does the empty display cabinet at the Ashmolean now contain, if not the Messiah?'

'My brother's imitation – a violin of no particular provenance or great value, worth three guineas at most.'

'So, they were swapped,' said Holmes, reclining in his favourite armchair, lighting his pipe and drawing in smoke, eager to learn more, to apply his brilliant brain to the problem at hand.

'Precisely. Look, I had no idea then that events should conspire to escalate a perfectly innocent act of friendship and brotherly trust into what could become a full-blown scandal.'

'How long do we have?' asked Holmes, puffing on his pipe, leaping from his chair and pacing up and down in front of the mantelpiece.

'Until Sunday night. On Monday morning, as fate would have it, the world-famous conductor Sir Henry Evans, along with a group of his orchestra, shall be visiting the Ashmolean specifically to view and play the instrument. The duplicate would be easily found out. Sir Henry also happens to be an expert on the Stradivarius, having written many well-received books upon the subject.'

'Humph – we have no more than two days at most. The trains will be running poorly due to all this snow, but it's worth a try.'

'What's worth a try?' said I, helping myself to more whiskey.

'While you were visiting Bradleys, my dear boy, Franzen provided me with certain crucial details that you are unaware of. In order to travel to his home in Kent, after school he catches a slow stopping service from Sydenham Hill in Dulwich through to Penge East and Penge West, his own stop being the one remaining station before Orpington – Clock House.'

'Yes, I'm with you.'

'It is on this singularly ordinary journey that he is certain the Stradivarius violin was brazenly stolen from under his very nose. Pray explain further, Mr Franzen.'

'That evening I finished my private music tutorial at six o'clock, long after the bell. I was teaching first-formers, young Harvey and Ethbertson, the rudiments of piano scales, and after made my way with the violin case tucked safely under my arm to Sydenham Hill station to catch my train. As usual I navigated a steep embankment of steps crossing over the iron footbridge and waited on the freezing platform for my passenger service to arrive round the curve from East Dulwich.'

'The scene is set, my dear Watson,' said Holmes, enjoying himself, leaning against the mantelpiece enthralled, peering out at the snow pattering against the window pane, heaps of it gathering upon the lintel.

Franzen continued. 'I waited for some five minutes, and all of a sudden was joined upon the lighted platform by a clerical gentleman wearing a camel-haired overcoat and fedora hat and also a tiny, plump lady in furs holding a string bag. They were neither of them from the preparatory school and had not attended the Christmas concert the day before. In plain words I had never seen either of them in my life. They were complete strangers to me. We were polite to one another and once the stopping service pulled in, the vicar sprang forward and opened the compartment door, allowing the lady in first and me afterwards. We took our seats and the door was slammed shut.'

'And the Stradivarius?'

'Safely in my possession, tucked under my arm. Being a musician I can appreciate the violin for its fine playing, its divine tone and the feel of the fretwork. The fact it happens to be worth a fortune is neither here nor there. My own violin is a Mullis and Stogner, bought from a music shop in Penge, which I have owned since I started teaching, and I prefer it to the Messiah. It's all down to the individual. Broadhurst on the other hand is a musical genius, and for him the Stradivarius makes a profound difference. He sweeps his bow across the strings and becomes a god. The result – heavenly music.'

'Thus, Watson, we are presented with a kindly vicar and a short, stout lady in furs. The two obvious suspects have taken their seats in the carriage, one to the left opposite Mr Franzen, the other over by the far window.'

'Indeed. I was sat somewhere in the middle.'

'Pray continue,' said Holmes, relighting his pipe.

'I was offered by the lady a delicious pineapple sweet. A favourite confection of mine, and as the train steamed into Sydenham tunnel I popped it gratefully into my mouth.'

'With sudden and dramatic consequences.'

'Yes, I instantly became unconscious of my surroundings and lost all awareness of time and space. When next I awoke, we were clearing the tunnel and approaching Penge East Station, the platform in evidence.'

'And the two other passengers?'

'Sat exactly where they had been before. The cleric, a somewhat childish, naïve expression on his face, the woman sucking on her own sweet, busy knitting a colourful scarf, both of them oblivious to my wretched predicament.'

'Which was?'

'The violin was nowhere to be seen. It had vanished. Horrified, I got up and began searching the luggage rack, the floor, beneath the seat cushions. I was frantic with worry. "Are you all right dear?" said the woman, looking up from her knitting as we rolled into the station. "I've lost my violin!" I blurted out. On the surface both my fellow passengers seemed perfectly composed and were only too willing to offer assistance. He, the vicar, instantly removed his overcoat and rolled up his sleeves, making a minute search of the compartment. She removed her fur coat and got down on her knees, searching every inch of the floor, but all to no avail, for the violin had been stolen, of that I was certain. Some sort of subterfuge was underway and I was convinced the vicar and the woman were working together as a team.'

'How can you be so quick to blame the vicar or the lady in furs?' said I, sensing a discrepancy.

'No sooner had our train departed Penge East than, like a pair of carrion crows, they proceeded to peck away at my confidence. "Are you certain that you did not inadvertently mislay the violin case – leave it on a bench, forget to pick it up when the train came in, forget to check the waiting room at Sydenham Hill station?" "Stop!" I screamed, by now hysterical, practically tearing my hair out. "The violin was with me when I entered the carriage to take my seat. The violin case was tucked under my arm thus." Still the vicar with his compassionate manner and holier than thou airs introduced doubt after doubt.

'The woman too persisted to humour me, showering me with her clever suggestions of how I might check with lost luggage at Victoria, make an enquiry to the station master at Sydenham Hill. Anyhow, by now the train was at Clock House. I clambered out of the carriage, certain it was they who had stolen the violin. There can be no other logical explanation.'

'But it was not concealed on their persons,' said I. 'They both removed their coats, did they not? The woman only carried a string bag and they had no other luggage.'

'Surely my dear Watson you shall have judged the couple guilty by now.'

'Why on earth should I?'

'My dear fellow, surely it is obvious,' said Holmes.

'So far I have heard not one jot of evidence that convinces me of their guilt.'

'The pineapple sugar sweet.'

'What?' I ejaculated.

'It was tainted by someone with pharmaceutical knowledge. A precise measure of sleeping draught added before the sticky mixture was moulded into a chunk and smothered with sugar.'

'Of course Mr Holmes, why, I had never thought of that,' admitted Mr Franzen, clapping his hands excitedly. 'It makes perfect sense.'

'I should agree that the overbearing nature of the vicar's godliness, and the annoying prattle of the lady in furs, implicate them in some form.

Unfortunately, as Doctor Watson has already pointed out, the evidence would not prove conclusive in a court of law. We none of us can avoid the fact that the violin was not to be found hidden on their persons, or stowed away in some shoulder bag or travelling portmanteau. In short, the violin was not in the compartment. So where was it?'

'I checked everywhere,' said the embittered music master. 'Everywhere. I am at a total loss.'

'Well, I believe the couple to be entirely innocent,' said I, puffing on my cigar. 'After all, the vicar appeared to have acted honourably, behaving with a good deal of compassion.' The lady likewise I felt was being wrongly accused.

Mr Franzen could not contain his emotion any longer. Tears were welling in his eyes. 'Mr Holmes, I'm counting on you. I and my brother face ruin and humiliation, a loss of career prospects and a lengthy prison sentence.'

'I understand,' answered Holmes, smiling weakly and patting the old fellow's shoulder. 'A train journey seems unavoidable if we are to successfully solve this most pressing of cases. Watson, be a good fellow and pass me that copy of Bradshaw's will you?'

The timetable board at Victoria announced numerous cancellations due to the inclement weather. Trains to Kent, however, were not too badly affected, being a half hour or an hour delayed before departure. At Herne Hill our stopping service to Beckenham Junction was held up by frozen points and a continuous stop signal, but once we got moving, although the train was slow, we eventually managed to reach East Dulwich and carry on round the curve to Sydenham Hill. On our journey Mr Franzen smoked cheroots, while myself and Holmes declined and settled for cigarettes. What a shame, I thought, that this kindly tutor, so attuned to his love of music and a veritable mine of information concerning composers, Wagner in particular, should have suffered such a blow. The police in Oxford should take a very dim view of his antics concerning the Messiah violin, and he and his brother would certainly be in for the high jump should he be found out. Time was of the essence and as our train pulled into the snowy platform, beside a long sweep of iron railings upon which was displayed advertisement boards, he looked a worried man with much on his conscience.

Once we had disembarked, we waited for what seemed an age on the exposed platform while Holmes strolled up to the end and studied the sooty orifice of the tunnel situated just beyond the steps of the iron footbridge. He paced up and down and peered over the edge at the wooden sleepers and ballast.

The next stopping service to Penge East arrived alongside the platform and, anxious to escape the cold wind we were glad of at least a sheltered compartment. We bundled inside, grateful for our seats and, not long after the train pulled out, we entered the Sydenham tunnel.

Forced back by the swaying motion of the carriages and the rush of air from the hollow vacuum of the musty tunnel, leaning out of the window Holmes barely managed to avoid being beheaded for at that instant a train rattled past in the opposite direction. Such was the closeness of the two trains as they slowly passed each other in the narrow tunnel that I could clearly see the passengers in the adjacent compartments reading their newspapers and chatting to one another.

'So there are two sets of track inside the tunnel,' mused Holmes, slumping back into his seat. 'The up- and the down-line trains pass one another midway. The trains are both slow stopping services, not expresses, and the possibility of transferring the violin case by some method of wire hook from one carriage to another remains a distinct possibility.'

'Extraordinary,' ejaculated the music teacher.

'Thus we have a third party, an accomplice,' said I. 'You infer that while the two sets of carriages passed one another in the tunnel, the violin case was transferred from one open compartment window to the other.'

'Precisely, my dear fellow. Thus when Mr Franzen awoke from his drug-induced nap, the violin case was nowhere to be seen. In effect, no amount of searching would ever find it for it was gone – vanished. But what I should like to know is who was this other accomplice, the person who waited so astutely in the down-line carriage with his metal hook implement at the ready, waiting for the vicar to transfer the violin case through the open window? I must confess, Mr Franzen, I now have my suspicions concerning your brother. Could he possibly have had anything to do with the planning of this robbery of the Messiah?'

'Outrageous! I would not countenance such speculation. He is the curator of the Ashmolean, his reputation as a scholar and academic unblemished. Like me, Mr Holmes, he is naturally interested in the Messiah as an instrument of historical significance. But as to its monetary value or rarity, he cares little. No, I'm afraid Edward cannot be first on your list of suspects. This accomplice you talk of, the third party as it were, is I fear for now someone completely unknown to us.'

'Let us pause to consider old ground,' said I. 'Who exactly knew of the loaning of this violin?'

'Why, my brother, myself and young Broadhurst. None other.'

'Well, if we eliminate yourself and Edward from the list, that leaves only one person remaining.'

'The young boy? A second-former? Oh, come now Doctor Watson, the very idea is far too fanciful.'

'And yet, it is not so preposterous,' admitted my companion. 'His fame at the school Christmas concert may have turned his head. Perhaps in his mind the musical genius now considered the Messiah his own, his alone to work his magic with.'

'Ha ha, Mr Holmes, we are now entering the realm I fear of the evil fairy of the Christmas pantomime. Young Broadhurst did indeed covet the violin and told me of his extreme attachment to it and longing to play it on a regular basis. But he is a mere schoolboy. Harmless, and yet...'

'Capable of stealing the instrument.'

'Totally in respect of his esteemed music teacher, Doctor Watson. His gratitude knew no bounds when he handed it back to me after the concert.'

'But you brought it to school regularly.'

'I never let it out of my sight. Wherever I went the violin came too.'

By now the train had emerged from Sydenham tunnel and we were passing the goods yard and rows of terraced houses before entering Penge East station. The locomotive hissed and panted into the platform, where we alighted, the time being by the station clock a quarter past eight. It was dark and biting cold. Flurries of snow blew along the station forecourt, and the pavements were icy underfoot. We stood in the shelter of the ticket office.

'Tell me about young Broadhurst,' said my companion, lighting a cigarette. 'Not his exquisite violin playing, but rather his personal life.'

'The boy is orphaned Mr Holmes, and lives with his uncle and aunt here in Penge in Larch Grove. I have never met his relations and they were unable to attend this year's Christmas concert, but he speaks highly of them. The family, according to the school bursar, are quite hard up, but then who isn't these days.'

'Larch Grove, you say.'

'I recall Broadhurst mentioned that he strolls through the park on his way to school. We can reach his home by crossing the main road that leads into Penge.'

'Mr Franzen, may I be so bold as to suggest we pay an impromptu visit to your pupil's home? Oh, now don't concern yourself, the meeting shall be informal and entirely on cordial terms with the boy. I only ask that you pay special attention to the uncle and aunt, for I strongly suspect you shall recognise certain of their characteristics. If you do, simply cough loudly thrice and I shall thereafter proceed with some gentle questioning. If nothing is amiss, why we shall raise our hats, wish the family the compliments of the season and be on our way. However, on no account act irrationally or become embroiled in some violent argument. Leave the interrogation to me and above all remain composed and dignified at all times.'

'Very well,' answered the music teacher, a whimsical expression upon his features. 'We were just passing, and being the end of term I wanted to call on my pupil and wish him and his family a merry Christmas. I understand your deception.'

'Excellent. You on the other hand, my dear Watson, must keep your gaze firmly fixed upon the boy and watch his every reaction. Three loud and hearty coughs is all that is required, Mr Franzen. No hysterics.'

'Very well, you have my word Mr Holmes.'

Walking at a brisk pace past the church with its tall steeple we crossed the busy main road and entered the park. At least a further inch of snow had fallen in the last half hour and it was dark and dismally cold. Passing an open expanse of ground blanketed in white, we came to a set of wrought iron gates which led us out of the park and into a neat cul-de-sac of terraces. Broadhurst's house was the fifth along and as the front gate clanged and we trundled up the garden path to the font door, I saw through the lighted window a family group taking tea.

My companion knocked at the door with the end

of his cane, a sharp rap that no one along the little street could fail to hear.

A gentleman of middle years answered the door, dabbing his chin with a napkin.

'Good evening,' said Holmes, politely removing his silk top hat. A tubby, round figure of a woman now came to the door and it was at this point that Mr Franzen went very red in the face and began a fit of coughing.

'You appear to have a chest infection, Mr Franzen. Does something ail you?' asked Holmes, a wicked gleam in his eye.

'I have now recognised I am standing in front of the same vicar and the lady in furs who shared a carriage with me from Sydenham Hill to Clock House earlier this week,' said he, glowering at the pair.

'Master Broadhurst,' called out my companion, 'do you really want your devoted music master to spend the rest of his days breaking rock and oakum picking in Pentonville Prison after being charged with theft?'

'N– no sir.'

'Of course not. Then be a good fellow and fetch the Messiah from beneath your bed, along with the hook contraption you used so effectively to snare the violin case from a moving train midway through Sydenham tunnel. Be brisk, for with luck Mr Franzen shall be able to return the priceless instrument to Oxford tonight. There is a late-running milk train which departs London at eleven-twenty and it is imperative for both his and your future happiness that he is on it.'

I heard footsteps scamper on the staircase and not long after a boy pushed his way between his anxious-looking relatives and offered both the violin and a spring-loaded telescopic rod with a queerly bent coat hanger on the end for Holmes's closer scrutiny.

'Tell me, madam,' said he, testing the spring-loaded arm that snapped back and forth, 'You were once employed in a pharmacy, I believe?'

'I still am, sir', she said proudly. 'I work for R. Bentley along Penge High Street.'

Wiping her hands on her flowery pinafore the woman seemed embarrassed by the fierce way Mr Franzen was staring at her. I am sure that had it not been for the presence of myself and Holmes on that freezing doorstep, the music teacher should have reached out and tried to strangle her with his bare hands, for he was no doubt recalling her kind offer of the pineapple sweet and the soporific effect it had had on him.

'An explanation is in order,' said Holmes, returning the ingenious device to the young lad.

'It's all Paganini's fault,' the boy burst out. 'For he used this same wondrous violin at many concerts and it was widely believed he was possessed of the devil when he played. I can only tell you I became obsessed, mesmerised by the violin and could not bear to part with it. I would have done anything to play it again. What insufferable madness, what insanity of reason took me over – Paganini's the Devil, I'm sure of it.'

'We must thus presume that the best and most secure place for the Devil's violin is surely under lock and key, returned to its own curio cabinet at the Ashmolean. However, I have an interesting proposition to make.'

'Really?' said the pretentious child, already so grown up, his serious expression somehow incongruous with being a mere nine-year-old.

'You know, as Doctor Watson here will confirm, my brother Mycroft purchased the Viotti Stradivarius of 1709 from an old acquaintance of his at the Diogenes Club. A rash fellow who, having incurred a number of heavy gambling debts and requiring urgent funds, decided to sell. My brother himself, a keen lover of opera and ballet, could I am sure be persuaded to pass the said Viotti on to me. Well, being Christmas week, I propose I loan you the instrument for next term in order that you may achieve the scholarship Mr Franzen talks of so earnestly.'

'A Stradivarius, a Viotti. Oh that's wonderful news.' The precocious child could not help but smile, his heart brimful of joy.

While snowflakes swirled about the lamp-lit porch, the boy's aunt and her husband hugged one another and drew the boy closer. The tableau of a happy family could not be more complete.

'Why, that's most generous of you Mr Holmes,' said Franzen, all hurt feelings and recriminations forgotten, beside himself with pride for his young prodigy, knowing full well my friend's Viotti Stradivarius could secure Broadhurst's reputation in the music establishment and eventually help him become a world-renowned concert and recording artist.

Without further delay, for he had a train to catch, the Dulwich music teacher raised his hat and wished us a merry Christmas, before hurrying on his way to Oxford.

3

The North American Speaking Tour

The fame of my friend Mr Sherlock Holmes had spread well beyond these shores and in his latter years he undertook a series of speaking engagements on a lecture tour offered him by the American theatre agent Erling Marks. For an incredible sum of money he agreed with some reservation to publicly speak about his advanced methods of detection and touch upon the process by which he solved a number of both fascinating and problematic cases.

The agent also specified there should be at least one gruesome murder discussed per lecture accompanied by lantern slides.

Our first engagement was for the Association Hall in New York and I confess I was delighted to accompany my dear friend on his travels of the Unites States and Canada. We left Liverpool in the luxury Cunard liner *Parthia* in mid-October and berthed in New York several weeks later. I should explain that both of us were hardy and fit and a winter tour held no particular fears for our health.

The agency was responsible for my esteemed colleague's every whim and comfort. I merely attended to his simpler needs, such as making sure he always had a plentiful supply of his favourite shag tobacco, that English cheese, pickles and mustard were on hand and that the meals were to his taste. The reader will of course know of our enthusiasm for fine dining, Simpsons of Piccadilly and Marcini's Italian restaurant being two of our great favourites when eating out after a concert.

We preferred to keep to our cabin for most of the trip, and the stormy forecast for the Atlantic crossing proved more than accurate. The ship heaved and dived, the rain lashed against our porthole windows and walking on deck was more akin to walking the plank, such was the ocean swell – a risky business undertaken only occasionally.

While Holmes avidly read a number of forensic tomes kindly forwarded by Miriam Lehmann, the other partner in the agency who was based in Manhattan, I kept to my military adventures. I had a stash of penny novels on the voyage and the rough seas and stormy weather only enhanced my enjoyment.

Lady Fleming, a young woman of Scottish descent who was in a cabin three doors down from us, would insist on bringing her pet spaniels along to meet us, and the little pups caused much merriment, although they were overly fond of nipping ankles and dragging out socks from under the bed.

The family history of Lady Fleming's husband deserves special mention, for his grandfather knew Mark Twain as a young man and in 1858 worked as a steersman on board the New Orleans–St Louis packet *The Mississippi*. He later invested modestly in the then budding coal and oil fields of Pennsylvania and made a fortune out of his stake. Thereafter he moved to Canada, invested in railway stocks and made further profits.

However, he ended his days as a trapper working for the Hudson Bay Company, learning all the skills of hunting and fur trapping, living in the northern wilderness in a log cabin. By the time he was killed in a drunken brawl in the city of Yellowknife over fur skins by an Iroquois Indian, he was worth in excess of $800,000, which in turn passed by way of inheritance to his son, now Lady Fleming's husband Jack, who himself resided comfortably for part of the year in Ottawa. Hence her ladyship's first-class passage to New York on Cunard's finest ocean-going liner.

Canada being second only to Russia in size, a vast country that spreads over nearly 4 million square miles, with all the wonders of the Northern Territories, the mountain ranges and the Great Lakes, the agent Marks had written into our contract only one mode of transportation – the train, and the Grand Trunk Railroad.

When the final contracts for the speaking tour were signed I recall both Holmes and myself studied the hefty fifty-page itinerary outlining the hectic schedule to be adhered to at all costs in order that the maximum amount of tickets could be sold and politicians, police chiefs, famous personages and so forth could meet him backstage for publicity purposes.

Young Lady Fleming was offered complimentary tickets to attend the first lecture in New York City, and also some sold-out venues in Canada, and was delighted to accompany us.

I confess that her enthralling stories concerning

her husband's Scottish ancestry, along with her playful pooches, helped while away many a happy hour on board the ship that would otherwise have become, in short, tedious and something of a trial due to the stormy crossing, the violent motion of the boat, the inability to stand on deck due to storm-force winds and an almost continuous spray of seawater, dampening clothing and spirits alike. A day or two of rough weather is stimulating but after a fortnight of continuous howling gales and creaking of the ship's bulkheads, one starts to tire of it. Therefore it was with some enthusiasm that we learnt from the ship's bursar that our fellow passenger from the Highlands in Scotland was in fact booked into the same hotel as us, The Westminster on East 16th Street, and would be travelling on *The Indian Chief* with us up to Canada.

After berthing at New York Harbour and being checked through customs, we took a cab to the Westminster Hotel and were greeted in the lobby by Erling Marks, a pushy New Yorker who, along with his business partner Miriam Lehmann, had formed the legendary film production company Lehmann–Marks, which was also a distribution chain owning picture houses all over America. The reader can no doubt recall the many silent classics and the marvellous actors accompanying them. Lilian Gish and Harold Fielding I believe took a starring role in *The Forbidden Temple*, which broke box office records on both sides of the Atlantic. Well, the success of these independent films owes much to Lehmann–Marks as they were both talented partners and knew how to turn an honest buck.

'Why Mr Holmes, I guess they told you the city of Toronto barely gets three hours of daylight in November.'

Marks chomped on the end of his fat cigar; the closely cropped bullet head, the ruddy complexion, the loud checked Oxfords he wore, held up with vivid red braces, made me recoil.

'My dear Erling,' said Holmes, 'provided I have all the latest editions of the newspapers in my room and an ample supply of cigarettes and tobacco, I shall want for nothing. My needs are simple. I do not share the tourist's tireless quest to see the sights – the Great Lakes and so forth. I care not whether Toronto remains shrouded in darkness and icebound the entire year.'

The agent slapped my companion on the shoulder and laughed heartily. 'I can see you and me are going to get along just fine, Mr Holmes,' he chuckled. 'Your rooms await – the Presidential Suite. I trust it is to your liking gentlemen. If you want anything I shall be in room 901 directly beneath your own.'

'You will call us when our cab arrives? We have the rest of the afternoon off. I believe Holmes wishes to go over his script.'

'Everything is taken care of, Doctor Watson.'

I noticed Lady Fleming gaily wave her kid glove in my direction as she checked in at the Westminster's lavish reception desk. Her baggage was being transferred upstairs by means of an Otis lift and she mouthed the words 'see you later' to which I nodded.

'Crowds are already forming right round the block at the Association Hall,' said our charming valet,

Alexander. 'Full house. I guess Mr Sherlock is going down a storm.' 'Well, I'm glad to hear it,' I answered.

Once installed in our suite of rooms I observed my companion was irritable, and could not settle. Nothing was said but I strongly suspected that crossing the Atlantic had taken its toll and my friend was worn out and just wanted to rest for a couple of hours. This was the first indication of the immense strain being put upon his nerves. However, usage of the cocaine bottle and the syringe carefully placed in its leather case was not an option, and I was determined he should not partake of dangerous stimulants. Through his published cases many admirers thought they knew my companion intimately, like a close friend or a favourite uncle. In truth, I believe he felt alien to them and even before his first lecture on the speaking tour was having doubts.

'This is my first and last speaking tour, Watson,' he confided. 'I am a practical sort of fellow, who likes nothing better than applying my intellect to a fresh case, not regurgitating stale old memories to an audience of theatre-goers who lust only after the macabre and the sensational.'

Well, it's good to relate that after smoking his pipe, reclining in a comfy armchair upholstered in red satin and basking in front of a roaring log fire in the open grate, thereafter enjoying a luncheon of beefsteak, soft shell crabs and sweet champagne, my companion's gloomy outlook towards his North American tour changed dramatically. He was much more positive and preparing to go out to entertain the people.

By now baskets of flowers and fruit, and cards

and letters of congratulation were arriving constantly and there was a knock at the door every two minutes. We received a charming card and bouquet of gardenias from Lady Fleming which took pride of place on the mantelpiece. We had agreed to rendez-vous with agent Marks and discuss the seating plan of the theatre, and go over a few outstanding points concerning the lantern slide part of the show. I recall I was filling my pipe with tobacco, about to enjoy a relaxing smoke, when I heard a loud if somewhat muffled bang. The noise succeeded in startling our maid, Ruth, although Alexander paid little heed and continued polishing the glasses behind the bar. Two more bangs rang out. Holmes calmly turned the pages of the *New York Times*. The maid started to scream, which irritated him enormously.

'Calm yourself woman,' he said, beckoning me over. 'I expect it's locked air in a pipe, a faulty gas geyser in the bathroom below. One strikes a match and – boom! Help yourself to fruit or cigarettes my dear, there are plenty in the tin, untipped or filtered.' He paused to whisper in my ear, 'Watson, that was a Colt '45, a large handgun. We'd better go downstairs, we have a couple of hours to spare after all before the cab arrives for the speaking engagement. Wasn't agent Marks meant to be up here by now to go over the presentation?'

'Marks is situated in the suite below us,' said I, ominously.

By the time we reached the base of the staircase, sparkling with gilt mirrors and chandeliers, we had already guessed the awful truth. Erling Marks was dead – and this was only confirmed when some moments later a distraught waiter rushed out of suite 109 holding a blood-soaked fluffy towel close to his chest. The hotel's name, Westminster, was somewhat obliterated by crimson splashes of blood, and top officials and management quickly formed along the already crowded corridor.

'The police have been called,' said the manager, sombrely.

'May I?' said Holmes, coming forward, neatly sidestepping the glistening trail of blood that led across the Persian carpet to the prone and very dead body of the theatre agent. He had been shot several times. The back of his head was severely damaged and I knew as a practising physician that the wounds were fatal and the man was beyond help.

'Step back, I'm his business partner!' we heard a hoarse, gravelly voice call out. A distinctive Bronx accent, a New Yorker born and bred, I correctly surmised.

'Get out of the way, let me through! So they finally nailed you, eh Erl?' she practically spat out the words. 'Those darned Italians, should 'a paid 'em like I told yer. Jeez, what a mess.'

Suddenly realising that two of her clients were present in the room, she was all smiles. 'Say, Mr Holmes, Doc Watson, sure am glad to meet you. Name's Miriam, I'm Erl's partner. The show goes on, as they say.'

'Well, good evening,' I said, amazed by her lively assessment of what was a murder scene. My concerns were irrelevant, however, for she hurriedly shoved us both out of the door and led us back upstairs to our suite as though nothing had happened and the corpse of the agent lying in a pool of blood was only a dream.

I adored Miriam from the first time I saw her. She was a whirl of energy, feisty, a tireless talker, a superlative wit and above all adorable to look at. However, I digress. She managed to charm both myself and Holmes into almost forgetting about the murder downstairs, concentrating instead on the sold-out speaking tour engagement. Consulting the programme I saw it started at 8 p.m.

'I warned him,' she said, clutching onto my arm as we hurtled across Union Square in the cab. 'The Sicilians wanted a hefty cut, up to 50 per cent of the take. Erl had set up a chain of picture houses on the West Side. "That's our turf" they says, "stay out of Hoboken." Next thing you know – kaput – Erl's dead, an' I got me a real problem. Ah, here we are, gents, can you believe it, Sherlock Holmes's name up in lights – savour the moment – enjoy.'

Inside the theatre the house lights dimmed and the audience at Association Hall became hushed and expectant. The odd cough, a nose being blown, the movement of restless bodies on seats, but then on came Mr Sherlock Holmes to deafening applause. He stood upon a platform before a lectern, bathed in an eerie glow, a mixture of yellow and green spot lamps directed towards him. He appeared to me like some waxwork from Madame Tussaud's

45

Chamber of Horrors, which presumably was the desired effect.

Unlike Charles Dickens, my friend was neither a particularly lively nor dynamic speaker. He seemed ill at ease and had trouble reading the script. Most of the time he stood like a shop window mannequin, tense and immovable, his left hand resting on the lectern while the other he kept behind his back.

I looked around and saw a few people nodding off, but generally the attention levels of the audience were good, especially when the lantern slides began to appear on the white backdrop. The audience livened up considerably. I even heard a couple of ladies gasp at the loathsome image of a gaunt and very dead Charlie Peace, the photograph taken directly after he had been cut down from the gallows, the burn marks of the hemp rope, still clearly visible round his scrawny neck, looming large upon the screen.

This was all grist to the mill so far as the agency was concerned, and the emphasis on the macabre during the latter part of the lecture worked admirably, preventing a slump in interest and a disappointing finale.

Typical headlines the following morning read:

New York Herald: 'A chilling evening spent with the Master Detective.'

New York Daily Tribune: 'Holmes – so far unrivalled in the art of criminal detection – a remarkable evening spent in the company of greatness.'

New York Times: 'Mr Holmes speaks most eloquently upon the grisly subject of gas light murders.'

All in all it was not a bad evening, not spectacular or particularly memorable, but neither was it a failure, and my esteemed companion was to be congratulated on his firm resolve to see it through and give the audience value for money.

Miriam was delighted and had only praise for the first lecture of the tour. Lady Fleming assured him that things could only get better and first night nerves were to be expected.

Afterwards we attended an official dinner and reception given by the British Ambassador at the Arcadian Club. The following evening Holmes's second engagement was in Albany, going on from there to speak at Troy, Syracuse and Philadelphia before returning to New York, where we would board *The Indian Chief* Baldwin engine No. 60, an American built locomotive hauling twelve carriages including caboose, saloon, dining and observation cars. We would travel from Penn Station through Buffalo, Rochester, then on to Toronto via the East Coast Canadian Pacific Railroad.

Difficult to conceive, but by the spring of 1883 Canada was a country with but half a transcontinental railroad between Port Moody and Ottawa. Much money and labour was invested to create the railway we know today.

I will be perfectly honest here. Such was the frenetic pace of our schedule that we had little or no time to recuperate or recharge our batteries, let alone speculate on the recent murder of the theatre agent Erling Marks at the Westminster Hotel. By the time the police were involved we were long preoccupied with travel arrangements. Being awoken from our comfortable beds in the middle of the night and hustled yet again to the station to catch a train, we left our hotel in Union Square hardly knowing where we were in the world. I could barely recall whether a celebrity dinner attended by the top crime writers of America had been held in Albany or Syracuse, or if Holmes had been presented with a gold pipe at Troy or Philadelphia. One speaking engagement seemed to blur into another. By the time we had been wrenched from our beds for the fifth consecutive night at some unholy hour and taken to Penn Station to board *The Indian Chief* for Toronto, I hardly knew if I were dreaming or awake.

Holmes I knew to be suffering. He appeared to me pale and half dead, barely able to string a sentence together, unless revived by several cups of strong coffee. Surely the express was luxurious and the berths first rate, but the unremitting travelling from one city to another was grinding us both down, leaving us tetchy and our tempers frayed, and when I shaved in a bathroom mirror I was shocked to discover that I looked as if I had aged ten years.

Miriam seemed to me to thrive on stress and looked more lovely and vivacious than ever. She always kept busy, knew every detail of the schedule, ticket sales, who we would be meeting and where. I envied her, for her vitality put us to shame, but she assured me the trick was to take regular naps and reduce one's intake of alcohol, not increase it, as I had done often, sharing half a bottle of whiskey with Holmes before bed and various bottles of wine with our dinner.

Then came a dramatic turn of events, an incident in the dining car. Miriam collapsed at the table, the whites of her eyes clearly visible, her head lolling from side to side. How glad I was Holmes was sat beside me, for in a crisis he excelled and seemed to come alive, his sharp brain able to react quickly and decisively to an emergency without getting into a panic or becoming flustered.

Miriam, I recall, toasted Holmes's sold-out performances, draining her flute glass of champagne before starting her meal of braised Pacific salmon. We were all eating, enjoying the excellent cuisine of the dining car, and I was for once feeling talkative and a trifle more energetic than usual. Holmes and I were sticking to Indian mineral water, preferring to stay sober, and avoiding the fine French wines on offer.

Suddenly, Miriam grabbed her stomach and keeled over. As a doctor I realised the danger of the situation and held her head back in order to keep her airway clear and make sure her tongue did not choke her. My companion took one look at our dear agent and forced a quantity of salt down her throat.

'What on earth are you doing, Holmes?' said I, furiously.

'Antimony else arsenical poisoning, my dear fellow. Her flute of champagne was laced with poison. The reaction concurs, a couple of minutes or so before an utter collapse.'

He shoved her head this time forwards, slapping

her face several times. Miriam gurgled, her eyes flickered open and the salt, now a saline solution, took immediate effect. A number of waiters and Miss Dolly, our dear maid on the train, came to her assistance, for Miriam was violently nauseous and appeared very weak. But, I am glad to relate, at least alive. Thanks to Holmes's lightning reaction her life had been saved, the poison cleaned from her system before any real damage could be done, else a state of coma induced. After a short nap in her berth she made a full recovery and was back to her normal energetic self.

The Indian Chief was making good progress, the locomotive steaming through Canada's snowy wastes. But both myself and Holmes had suffered a relapse and were back to our old ways, drinking more than was good for us. Needless to say, I longed for a comfortable hotel and a proper bed for the night, to escape the constant motion of the train.

The saloon car was always packed. Tonight was especially lively, the smoky atmosphere conducive to wiling away many an hour, a Joplin ragtime tune was being thumped out on the ivories, the pianist first rate. Lady Fleming was dancing wildly, gyrating to the jazz beat. Miriam sat drinking glass after glass of neat Bourbon on ice, tapping her foot in time to the infectious rhythm.

She was fully recovered, and had put her fainting fit in the dining car down to indulgence. Neither Holmes nor myself had explained that she had been deliberately poisoned – until now that is.

'Please,' said Holmes, grey-faced from lack of sleep. 'Alas my dear Miss Lehmann, we are dealing with a man of possibly Sicilian extraction who is presently travelling on the train with us to Toronto. As you have correctly intimated, Erling Marks was murdered at the Hotel Westminster on East 16th Street by a gangster, to use the modern euphemism, paid I should imagine a considerable sum of money to do the job. Do you recall the distraught waiter emerging from room 109 with a bloodied towel, my dear Watson?'

'I do Holmes. The poor fellow must have been the first on the scene and witnessed the full horror.'

'Indeed, in fact he was the very first on the scene for it was he who shot Marks and left him for dead, the murder weapon, a Colt .45, cleverly concealed inside the soft towelling. Alas, everyone, including ourselves, fell for his clever ruse. He must have required nerves of steel though. I was so dreadfully lagged after the liner berthed at New York, my normally keen insight and ability to seize upon the facts had deserted me for I fell rather flat. I repeat, we have someone on the train who is intent on murdering Miss Lehmann and very nearly succeeded in the dining car.'

'You mean...,' she gasped.

'You were fortunate my dear. Had the dosage of antimony been more soluble in the champagne and dissolved quickly instead of crystallising at the bottom of your glass, you should have been dead by now.'

Miriam turned very pale, losing her normally effervescent bonhomie.

'It appears Marks formed only one part of the

contract, your pecuniary responsibility must be met forthwith Miss Lehmann.'

'A pay-off,' she muttered. Lady Fleming, who had now joined us, seized Miriam's hand in hers to offer comfort and support in her time of need.

'Precisely. Watson and myself will do our best to locate this Sicilian. An offer of $20,000 should suffice. If he refuses to cooperate and does not call the whole thing off our only option shall be to kill him and bundle his body out of the train. Presumably, my dear fellow, your service revolver was confiscated at the customs shed back at New York?'

'Indeed, Holmes. I even hold an official receipt.'

'Well, well, our bare hands must suffice. A kitchen knife or pyjama cord offer a more sophisticated option. Meanwhile, Miss Lehmann and Lady Fleming, it is imperative you remain here in the saloon car, in full view of everybody. On no account retire to your berths.'

I am glad to report we reached Toronto without incident. *The Indian Chief* pulled into Union Station and once out of that vast, imposing entrance hall we caught our first glimpse of the great city and in the early hours were taken by four-wheeler downtown to the Hotel Victoria. Holmes and myself had been unable to locate the Sicilian bounder responsible for trying to murder Miriam in the dining car. The person who shot Erling Marks dead was still at large, but I confess I was too tired to care. I slumped down on one of the leather sofas in the hotel lounge and ordered a pot of coffee. Our vivacious agent joined me, keeping me much amused with salacious tales of her clients in the silent film industry and what they got up to in the seclusion of their Beverley Hills mansions. Then she proposed a diversion.

'And of course John, I have saved the best until last.' She patted my knee teasingly. 'The Falls.'

'Niagara Falls,' said I, 'is perhaps not the most appropriate venue for sightseeing on our itinerary.' I reminded our agent of my companion's brush with death at the hands of Professor Moriarty. 'My view is that the fight to the death at the Reichenbach Falls remains firmly imprinted on my friend's subconscious. The trauma has never really left him, even now the sound of running water upsets him and he suffers spells of vertigo. I should not want a return to his black mood swings and over reliance on narcotic stimulants, cocaine in particular.'

'Like the rest of us, he must learn to face his fears,' she said brutally. 'He will never be able to move on otherwise. No wonder he is such an embittered old bachelor, set in his ways. But listen, John, what do I know, he's a genius for God's sake, the world's greatest consulting detective. I take it all back.'

'I think we should prefer something less arduous, a night at the opera house, a stroll around Toronto's gardens and parks, taking in a museum,' I suggested. 'Why, we could remain in Toronto for a day or two. The tour seems relentless to the extreme. We've hardly unpacked our bags before we are off again. Another city, another speaking engagement.'

'After Toronto we must return to Washington, John.'

'Already?' said I, frankly appalled. 'But we have only just unpacked. We have been on the go now since Philadelphia.'

I confess I should not speak ill of the dead but I complained in the strongest terms of how Erling Marks had arranged the scheduling for Holmes's 1908-9 tour, the pressure being placed upon him, the unrelenting cycle of interviews, crime club gatherings, charity dinners, meetings with the great and the good.

'Marks should have organised the tour better, cut the number of venues,' said I with feeling.

'You signed the contract.'

'Well, actually, Holmes did, but...'

'No buts, John. Now let's see, we have a luncheon engagement with Toronto's "Ladies of Baker Street". They are a club of ardent admirers, wealthy heiresses, top-notch socialites just dying to meet Mr Holmes – and yourself, of course.'

At that instant Lady Fleming breezed into the hotel lounge with her pair of spaniel pups, which provided a welcome diversion from talk of the tour. Not long after, poor Holmes arrived looking dishevelled, his hawk-like features grey and worn out, the front of his frock coat stained with soup. He was accompanied by two red-coated Royal Canadian Mounted Police wearing fur hats, and a plain clothes detective. I noticed Lady Fleming was about to reach into her handbag when one of the officers leapt forward and, to my astonishment, confiscated a Derringer pistol from her grasp.

'You're under arrest for the murder of Erling Marks, the impresario and theatre agent at the

Westminster Hotel in New York.' The detective placed a set of handcuffs round her delicate wrists. She remained defiant.

'Your maiden surname before marrying Lord Fleming of Moncrief and becoming part of the Scottish aristocracy?'

'Stenwick – Gloria Jane'.

'You are directly related to whom?'

'The film star Betty Stenwick.'

'Who died suddenly.'

'She committed suicide in Los Angeles three years ago.'

'Because?'

'*They* – Lehmann–Marks, would not renew her contract. She was effectively squeezed out of the studio. Their influence was such that no film company in L.A. would touch her. She was like damaged goods, her career in ruins the minute they – those filthy producers – decided to drop her. She was only twenty-six years old.'

'Betty Stenwick was finished,' snarled Miss Lehmann. 'Let me tell you Miss Goodie Two Shoes, she was addicted to morphine.'

'You're lying! You as good as killed her because she was having an affair with Erling and you didn't approve.'

'Ladies, please!' Holmes raised both hands in a gesture of conciliation. 'Miss Stenwick, I regret the loss of your sister in such tragic circumstances. A suicide is always hard to bear, but going round systematically murdering people is hardly the way forwards. Erling Marks, for all his faults, did not deserve to die at your hands. Back at the Hotel

Westminster, you cleverly disguised yourself as a waiter. I confess you had me completely fooled, even on *The Indian Chief* it was only after minutely searching your berth and discovering a photograph of Betty Stenwick, tucked behind the frame of which was a folded newspaper cutting, an article concerning your sister's tragic death in Los Angeles, that I became remotely suspicious.'

'You searched my berth?'

'I searched everybody's. The need to find the elusive assassin before he struck again was paramount. Miss Stenwick, you only have yourself to blame, carrying the same bloodied, fluffy towel clearly marked "Westminster" in your suitcase was surely a grave error on your part. It is all the evidence required to send you to the electric chair. I suggest you hire the services of a first-rate lawyer. There are mitigating circumstances. She was after all your sister and her unfortunate death must have upset you greatly.'

Lady Fleming, or should I say Gloria Stenwick, burst into tears and was led away by police to a waiting carriage outside the hotel.

I did my utmost to comfort Miriam, who was naturally upset, but to my astonishment she was soon hustling us out of the hotel lobby and calling for a cab, for it was already time to attend 'The Ladies of Baker Street' function in honour of Mr Sherlock Holmes.

4

The Watch-Mender

It was a quarter to twelve on a bright and sunny morning, with the crystalloid and surprisingly sharp frost of the previous night long since dissipated. Temperatures were sufficiently raised so that a fellow might pleasingly stroll about the West End without an overcoat, when our cab joined a steady stream of other carriages jostling along Regent Street.

Holmes was in fine fettle, his spirits uplifted, for he had received at breakfast a note from his brother Mycroft, requesting our presence at the Liberty department store at noon. We were to meet him in the furnishing section.

I recall that Mycroft liked nothing better than sifting around for Indian silk pyjamas, else choosing an exclusive William Morris block-print design to grace his flat in Pall Mall. Lunch at Simpsons was also on offer.

Hastening into the wood-panelled gallery, where groups of shopping enthusiasts were milling about, we hurried up the oak staircase to the overhead walkway, and thence to the furnishing department. And it was here that a very odd thing occurred, for there was suddenly a loud and ear-splitting *bang*.

At first, like other startled customers, we were confused at to cause, but then we observed an Oriental doll placed on top of an Art Nouveau sideboard of carved walnut beside a cloisonné enamel vase and Japanese blue and white tea jar. There was a large gaping hole in its chest and gunpowder smoke curling from the doll's clothing.

'My dear Watson,' said my companion, pointing his silver-topped cane firstly at the floor where there lay a spent brass cartridge case, and thence directing my gaze to a mark on the wall above the glass counter where a bullet had embedded itself in the plaster. 'Bizarre as this sounds, I believe we have just been shot at by that Oriental doll on top of the walnut sideboard.'

'An assassination attempt!' I replied, horrified.

'Just so. Let us enquire of that sales lady doing her best to calm everybody down from whence the deadly doll originates.'

We pushed through the throng of shoppers. Profuse apologies were being offered by staff for the noise and smell of gunpowder smoke still prevalent in the furniture department. The sales lady, a Miss Moss, dressed smartly in her Liberty gown, rushed over, pleased to answer any questions we might have.

The doll was apparently one of a batch delivered from Emily Pankhurst's shop in the East End – well known as a toy manufacturer. The labour force consisted entirely of poor, destitute women down on their luck, who welcomed the opportunity of being gainfully employed and earning a little extra money for bread. Neither of us for one moment suspected Emily or her workforce of being responsible for the assassination attempt; rather some clever fiend who had replaced the original with another identical doll, specially tinkered with to fire a single shot from close range while we happened to be walking past.

Mycroft, as the reader will appreciate, was nowhere to be seen. In fact he had been at his exclusive London club, the Diogenes, and had no knowledge of our lunchtime meeting, for the note we had received that morning was entirely bogus. We had been deliberately lured to Liberty's furniture department by someone intent on killing us. I recall a discrepancy concerning the note, for above Mycroft's forged signature was brushed a curious Chinese symbol of an eclipsed moon.

Being a sunny and crisp winter's day, after quitting the Tudor-fronted arts and crafts emporium, we decided upon a brisk trudge homewards to Marylebone, partly to clear out heads, partly to think things through and try to make sense of the events at Liberty. Neither of us had the faintest idea how the doll was operated, whether by a clockwork timing device, or trip-wire mechanism, but it had proved most effective and this was worrying.

Walking first to Oxford Circus and thereafter making our way along Great Portland Street, I confess that the feeling we were being followed did not abate. Crossing leafy Cavendish Square I paused to glance back over my shoulder, but could see nobody remotely suspicious. Later, in Wigmore Street, however, Holmes alerted me to a strange noise that can best be described as a pair of Dutch clogs, a wooden clacking sound as though an oversized marionette had been unleashed and was clumping along the street behind us.

We were shortly ensconced once more in the sitting room at our digs in Baker Street, in front of a roaring fire, I filling my pipe, Holmes perusing the latest editions of the newspapers before settling down to a light luncheon prepared by Mrs Hudson. I still found it hard to believe that my dear friend and room-mate, my trusted companion for so many years, should have been so nearly killed, let alone myself. I could not for the life of me shake off the annoying feeling that someone clever and articulate had managed to catch us with our guard down.

Such was our concern, Holmes telegraphed Inspector Lestrade at Scotland Yard, sharing the details of our experience at Liberty that morning. We hoped to hear from him soon.

However, it was not to be the Inspector who called later that afternoon but rather a police agent sent on his behalf, a native of Nanking Province, who had resided in the Chinatown area of Limehouse for most of his life. While working undercover for the police, Mr Choi had assisted in the arrest of many racketeers and gang-masters swarming the London docks. He was familiar with a number of infamous personages controlling the narcotics trade, the opium and gambling dens then rife in Limehouse. His watch included Wapping, Bermondsey, Poplar, Rotherhithe, Stepney, Deptford and the Isle of Dogs.

A pleasant fellow with a questioning turn of mind and an intense curiosity, he firstly wished to see the bogus note with the Chinese symbol brushed above Mycroft's forged signature.

'The assassin's mark, the eclipsed moon, denotes a swift death. Who on earth have you annoyed amongst the Chinese community?' said he, most puzzled.

'There can be only one explanation', said I, after much reflection.

'Go on.'

'Some years ago, we destroyed an opium factory down in Cornwall. Unfortunately a Mr Tong, in charge of the business, was fatally wounded during the course of events. His wife Lai Tong, a practising exponent of ju-jitsu, escaped justice.'

'Lai?' Mr Choi's eyes grew wide. 'Now I must tell you I am familiar with that name. She is a much feared and powerful Triad gang master, active in Limehouse and the East India docks. Obviously this is revenge for her husband's death. The attempt to kill you at Liberty will be but one of many. She has spies and informants who do her bidding.'

'The Chinese Triads, are you sure?' said I.

'Unfortunately that is the case.'

'But the attempt failed,' Holmes pointed out.

'This time perhaps,' said Choi, giving us both an inquisitive look.

'You would credit us that fate on this occasion intervened in our favour.'

'It appears that way, certainly. But to the sender of this note it is only a matter of time.'

'Dear me,' ejaculated Holmes, 'one feels not dissimilar I imagine to Marie Antoinette waiting hesitantly for Madame Guillotine's blade to fall. I trust you will share our humble repast of cold partridge temptingly displayed upon the sideboard, Mr Choi? Why, I think perhaps we shall uncork a bottle of best Burgundy to celebrate my imminent demise.'

'One more enquiry.'

'You only have to ask, Mr Choi.'

'Have you ascertained where the doll came from? The one you describe in the telegram to Lestrade?'

'A toy factory in the East End set up by Emily Pankhurst, the suffragette, in Ford Road, Poplar. Destitute young women, often penniless and in dire straits work there, glad of a chance to enjoy good, honest labour and a generously subsidised canteen. The doll you refer to was part of a batch delivered to Liberty with a consignment of wooden donkeys, monkeys and elephants.'

'Well, we must make the best use of our time. Let us check this place of toys tonight.'

Seldom have I encountered such a dense fog drifting off the Thames as upon the night of our excursion to Poplar. From Shadwell to Rotherhithe, West Ham to Hawksmoor's steepled church, the East End of London was engulfed in a filthy yellow miasma. As our hansom drove through the streets with its tinkling bell, the horses' hooves clopping upon cobblestones, we passed various dingy gin palaces and corner public houses – The Grapes, The Lighterman, The Stag and Hounds, all perceived fleetingly through poor visibility.

We eventually reached Ford Road and paid our

cab-man to stay in attendance. We alighted into a grim underworld of spectral shadows, the tinged glimmer from a row of streetlamps revealing a little shop with a window full of handmade toys.

'The factory is at the rear,' said Holmes, muffled up against the cold, clammy vapour of the fog. He produced his set of lock-picks. Mr Choi and myself followed the tall, spare figure of my friend round the back to a paint-flaked entranceway, a pasted variety hall advertisement adhering to the door.

Once inside the factory, the light shed by our lanterns highlighted uniform rows of work benches used by the ladies for the assembly and painting of wooden animals, and of course the range of Oriental dolls sold all over London. Strung above each bench was a wire on which were pegged toys in various stages of manufacture, requiring a leg or an arm or finishing painting. The smell of gloss paint and boiled gum for gluing pieces of wood together prevailed, but the place had a charming atmosphere, the women's loving attention to every detail of the process much in evidence.

'We must go,' said Mr Choi, seizing my arm, all of a sudden aware of some unpleasant sense of premonition.

'What are you talking about, man?' snapped Holmes, disgusted that the Chinese agent appeared to be in a state of panic.

'He's here, I can sense it.'

'Who, Mr Choi?' said I, staring into the darkness and wondering what on earth had come over him. 'To whom do you refer?'

'The assassin.'

'Nonsense.'

Then we all of us heard a dozen knitting machines start up – or at least that is what it sounded like. We froze, not daring to move. Mr Choi shone the beam of his lantern over by the workbenches but at the wrong height, for out of the gloom at skirting-board level came the real threat.

Rosy-cheeked dolls, their enamel painted eyes swivelling left to right, right to left, perfectly synchronised in the awkward motion of their stubby legs, advanced on us like a miniature army. But their permanent smiles were deceptive, for the automata would be merciless and show no quarter.

The first row began to blast away, intense flashing blue lights filling the small factory. Bullets were humming past, the skirting board behind us and the lower wall being shot to pieces.

Crouching behind a table I heard Mr Choi scream out. The poor fellow had been struck on the shin.

Somehow we all managed to get to the door and fled the place, I dragging the Chinese agent along the pavement. Even the fog was preferable to being fatally shot by a bullet. The sound of small arms fire could be heard halfway down the street.

'Are you badly hurt, Mr Choi?'

'Just a graze thank you, Doctor Watson,' said he, limping along. We hurried to the waiting cab and even as we left the toy factory behind, I could hear distant gunfire and observe the frosted factory windows flickering as though a thunder storm were raging inside.

Back at our lodgings in Baker Street I treated Mr Choi's flesh wound with a strong dose of iodine and a strip of bandage. Afterwards we took a stiff brandy each to calm our nerves before bed. I could not help but feel angry for once again we had been cleverly outwitted, subtly drawn into a trap, and it had nearly cost us our lives.

'What pestiferous toymaker conjured up those clockwork devils?' cursed Holmes. He was sat by the fire, looking despondent, counting the cost of a night's work gone badly wrong.

After a night on the couch the police undercover agent joined us at the breakfast table for a delicious repast of ham, egg and toast, and coffee prepared by Mrs Hudson. Breakfast finished, Holmes chose his old black clay from the rack upon the mantelpiece and filled it with stale dottles from the previous night's smoke. He slumped in his favourite fireside armchair and lamented.

'How I wish I knew who Lai employs as her proficient assassin, Watson. Another narrow escape, you must agree, my dear Choi nearly maimed for life.'

'I have been thinking,' said he. 'Last night I had a queer dream. I dreamt of someone completely unknown to me, a Chinese surrounded by countless clocks, a work table covered in instruments, a jeweller's eyeglass. This sounds uncanny, I know, Mr Holmes, but such a man exists.'

'He would be thus competent to manufacture automata.'

'Exactly,' said Choi, his eyes dancing with delight. 'I have never met him personally but Mrs Lu Lang from the laundry swears by him for repairs to watches and clocks and clockwork toys, and she is not the only person. "The Crab", as he is known, has a reputation in the area of Pennyfields and Limehouse Causeway for excellent workmanship. He is surely the person with the requisite skills and maturity of purpose.'

'Pray why do you refer to him as "The Crab"? said I, at a loss to understand.

'The watch-mender has an unlucky history, Doctor Watson. One winter's day at East India Docks, Chu Chin slipped on a puddle of ice and fell beneath the wheels of a horse-drawn train heaped with wine casks, advancing along the wharf's tramway. The injuries sustained were truly terrible, for he lost both feet.'

'How tragic,' said Holmes, puffing on his pipe, a rank fug of tobacco smoke drifting up to the ceiling.

'But there is more. When lying in hospital, weak and on the point of death, he called out for his brother Chi Chin and hastily drew a rough sketch and passed it to him. It was an invention that would help transform his life. By an arrangement of hollow metal poles, a special steel reinforced whalebone corset and flanged hinges affixed to a pair of wooden clogs, he would be able to walk again. His brother, a skilled metalworker, lost no time and manufactured the parts at home in his workshop. And when I say "walk again", I refer to a queer twisting motion, a crablike, sideways shuffle reliant upon the flanged clogs.

'To master this contraption it took a superhuman effort, the trauma of the accident alone must have been hard enough to bear, but what of Chu Chin's mental state of mind, the endless repetition, falling over countless times to activate locomotion, the hurt, the bitterness for the misfortune that through no fault of his own befell him? The burning hatred for his present predicament?'

'There lies the crux,' said I. 'The mind becomes warped, the obsessive nature of the slow recovery is redirected into his refined and clever toy-making. Why, he should actually over time start to live his life through those incredible automata.'

'So we can thereby assume,' interjected Holmes, 'that at some stage Lai Tong, now a powerful and respected gang-master, a dominant Triad force in Chinatown, befriends Chu Chin, gains his complete confidence, consequently helping him achieve his ambitions by turning him into a first-rate assassin, a demonic toymaker driven by a need to perfect and nurture his mechanical children.'

'But you did kill her husband, so part of the blame lies with you also,' Mr Choi insisted. 'Karma must inevitably run its course in our lives.'

'Only in the line of self defence,' said I, putting the record straight. 'Good Lord, Tong intended to riddle us full of bullets, a detective of police included, with a Gatling gun. It was only lucky he was distracted and I shot him in the head first.'

'But how do we resolve our present situation, I wonder?' asked Holmes, knocking out his pipe on the brass fireguard.

'Chu Chin must be eliminated.' Mr Choi spoke in a determined way. 'We must strike first or bear the consequences. It will be him or us, I cannot speak plainer.'

'But how on earth do we go about it?' said I, finishing my cigar.

'We must venture into Limehouse, but not as you are, Doctor Watson. The tightly knit community of Chinatown would be suspicious of a foreigner.'

'A disguise, my dear fellow. I have the very thing. A trunk-load of theatrical clothes from an amateur production of Gilbert and Sullivan's *Mikado*. Come Watson, the pigtail, black pill box hat, silk shirt and baggy trousers shall suit us admirably. That and a smidgeon of greasepaint. While we change, Mr Choi, help yourself to more coffee, the cigars are in the coal scuttle.'

The district known as Limehouse, east of Wapping and in sight of the docks, where the masts and spars of tall sail ships can be seen, and which includes Limehouse Causeway, Lime Kiln Docks and Pennyfields, has a justified reputation for crime and murder, for much illegal revenues are raised from opium and gambling and shared amongst the various Triad gangs there.

Holmes and myself had had cause to visit Chinatown in the past, and even now I shudder when I recall walking its dark streets at night, enduring the risk of being beaten by drunken Malay or Chinese sailors, else left for dead in some filthy gutter with my throat slit from ear to ear, fleeced of any personal possessions. Yet I must emphasise to the reader that the majority of residents are honest, hardworking individuals employed in the laundry and restaurant trades. That said, the ardent racketeer is always close at hand, eager to rough up, intimidate and demand protection money. That evening, as the freezing fog drifted off the Thames, disguised as a couple of Chinese traders, we walked back and forth along the main thoroughfare congested with over-burdened hand carts loaded with crates of squawking chickens, bags of rice and bales of silk, traipsing from one Chinese laundry to the other in search of any information leading us to the whereabouts of the watch-mender.

The old Chinaman behind the counter of the Huang Sung Laundry ate his bowl of noodles and paid little heed to our presence in his shop.

'You know of Lai Tong?' asked Mr Choi, not prepared to take any nonsense from the old man. 'You pay plenty good protection money, stay on best buddy terms, no?' The laundryman paused to contemplate a milky porcelain figurine of the *Kwan Yin*, the goddess of mercy, before him.

'I have heard it said Lai Tong is a *da huo*, a temporary partner to an overlord. I cannot say I am overly enamoured by her band of thugs who call each Saturday night and seize a quarter of my hard-earned takings.'

'And "The Crab"?', said Mr Choi, grinning and totally at ease with the laundryman.

'Ha! I know of whom you speak. Chu Chin, the watch-mender.'

'I have a poor old clock in need of repair, the mechanism run down, the hour hand a little lazy. You know that Mrs Chan from the Chung Li Laundry cannot speak highly enough of his workmanship, nor his excellent prices.'

'Then you will find him on weekdays at his little cell above the chandler's shop, not far from the main entrance to the East India docks. Chi Chin his brother helps out from time to time, although neither of them will be there today on account of business down Bermondsey way. Better luck tomorrow. Our rates are reasonable for washing and boiling sheets, there is nowhere along the High Street cheaper. Good day to you all.'

The short but most enlightening interview thus came to a close. As was the custom Mr Choi made a polite bow and hinted we should likewise pay our respects to the old Chinaman, who had no need for platitudes, and waved us away.

I was glad to escape the stifling heat of the washing vats and the steam from the presses, but then we each of us heard a loud clack of wood on wood, for the laundryman had perched himself on a tall stool to take the weight off his feet, or to be more precise, the weight off his heavy clogs. With a sinking feeling in the pit of my stomach I realised we were in the presence of none other than the treacherous assassin, "The Crab", but before Chu Chin could unleash a further army of mechanised horrors of what shape or form I had no idea, that accomplished toymaker, the Napoleon to his army of automata, fell back with a pained expression, a long curled dagger protruding from his chest.

'Die you devil!' cried Choi, marshalling us out of the laundry, looking anxiously this way and that, desperate that we should merge into the crowd. 'We must race like the wind! Some wretch working in the laundry will have by now alerted the Triads. We must somehow escape Chinatown, for Lai Tong will soon know that one of her closest confederates has been killed, and the district will be effectively sealed off, even the docks would not be safe.'

'But why the haste?' asked Holmes. 'Surely the fog off the Thames and the crowds of Chinese offer shelter from prying eyes.'

'It would have done,' answered Mr Choi bitterly, a note of total disdain in his shrill voice. 'But your disguises have slipped, Mr Holmes. Here, stop by the restaurant window and study your reflections.'

The awful truth dawned. The moisture and intense steam from the laundry had caused the greasepaint to run, our make-up to spoil. Our faces to the outside world now appeared vivid orange, streaked with rivulets of black hair dye. This meant we no longer resembled haughty traders but rather monsters from the fairground. The collar of my silk shirt was stained and filthy. I felt vulnerable. More than ever we were marked men. Even then I could hear rapidly approaching footsteps. Choi bustled us down a narrow alleyway.

'We must split up,' said he, shoving me along. 'If we are caught we shall be cut into small pieces and never be seen alive again. Never underestimate the Triads, Mr Holmes,' he said breathlessly, glancing behind him again and again, terrified we should be captured. 'There is a fork in the way ahead, Doctor Watson. Keep to the alley until you come out by the East India Dock. Myself and Holmes will cleave to the backs of the restaurants – we all end up at the same place. Best of luck.'

Luck! Mine was about to run out. I stumbled blindly through the fog, the cold clammy vapour soaking my clothes. I longed for my tweeds, my winter overcoat, my hat, a stout pair of walking shoes, rather than the wretched plimsolls Holmes had dug out from the trunk, but above all I pined for my old way of life. I felt all at sea, lost in a different culture, and then I saw a shadowy figure walk out in front of me. I immediately saw the resemblance. Of course, the watch-mender must have had considerable influence and being in the pay of Lai Tong meant his death would be swiftly avenged. The walls of Limehouse seemed to close in on me. I was in a cobbled square, hemmed in on three sides by dosshouses and tenements.

'We have a saying in Chinatown, Doctor Watson: – *Sha ji jing hou* ... It means "kill a chicken to warn and set an example to the monkey".'

'Presumably I am the chicken,' said I, not much liking what I perceived to be an open threat. 'You know, Chi Chin,' for I presumed this was he, 'your brother was a psychopath, hopelessly so, who gloried in his merciless automata, whose mind was warped long ago after his accident when he lost both his feet. Your fate does not have to be irrevocably linked with his, you do not have to embrace the gallows shed at Pentonville. Have you a wife and family? Consider your next move carefully.'

'And your beloved Mr Holmes is the monkey,' said he, not even listening, and taking a glittering metal star from his pocket and running his finger sensuously along the serrated edge. 'By eliminating you, his closest ally and dearest friend, he receives a severe and painful reprimand.'

'You still have an opportunity, use it wisely. You

still have time to board a ship for your homeland, a tea clipper, a lengthy voyage away from the East End.'

Here was I resembling the wandering minstrel from the *Mikado*, shaking in my boots, stalling for time. I knew I was presently facing another dangerous individual and my own time was running out. He raised his arm. I had no idea how to disable him. I'd left my service revolver at home. All I could focus on was that shiny metal star. There was a flourish of gunpowder smoke and a king-size firework rocket shot past my ear with a loud *whoosh*, impaling itself in the Chinaman's paunch. Chi Chin was thrown backwards by the sheer force of the rocket and fell heavily onto the cobblestones. His body continued to jerk and shudder a full five minutes while each progressive explosive charge ignited until all that was left of my immolated adversary was a smouldering heap of rags.

Sherlock Holmes and Mr Choi emerged from behind a wide refuse bin left by the restaurant which backed onto the alley. Mr Choi had a blackened terracotta drain pipe supported on his shoulder and looked very pleased with himself.

5

The Black Dog Conundrum

Consulting my notes for the year 1897, the name Mrs Munn once more appears upon the pages of my numbered journals. This formidable lady was a resident of Clapham who lived in a terraced house on the far side of the common, and was a keen spiritualist and practising psychic.

One morning, at the height of summer, we received a lengthy epistle from her youngest daughter Edie explaining that her mother had been laid low with influenza and although making a full recovery had asked after us often and wondered whether we might like to pay her a visit at Clapham. Holmes and myself had both grown very fond of this prescient if elderly lady, and needed little prompting.

We caught a train from Victoria and, after walking briskly from the station, my companion's coat tails flying and his silver-topped cane held jauntily over his shoulder, found ourselves once more on the threshold of her quaint little terrace. The door to her house was open, allowing summer sunshine to brighten the hallway. Holmes placed his top hat on the polished stand. The daughter greeted us and we were led to a light and airy back bedroom full of vases of colourful flowers and bowls of perfumed hyacinth.

Always a dominating presence, Mrs Munn lay in bed reading her Bible. While Edie plumped the pillows and made her comfortable, Holmes and myself settled into a pair of chintz-covered armchairs. A Londoner born and bred, a tough and resilient character who had seen much in her long life, Mrs Munn appeared warm and friendly until, quite unexpectedly, she sat bolt upright, her plump features all of a sudden wooden and corpse-like, her eyes rolling around in her head.

'Psychic fits come upon her, never to worry,' said Edie, gently wiping her mother's brow with a warm flannel. 'Ma sometimes comes over all queer like this. We just accept it, never does no harm, don't be a-worrying, gentlemen.'

After making a gurgling noise in her throat, Mrs Munn adopted a mediumistic guise and started to speak in a low voice. 'I see great dangers ahead for both of you,' she intoned, 'be wary of the diligent gardener lest he cuts you down.'

Thus was the unsettling message received from the spirit world. The trance-like state ended and, after a reviving cup of tea, Mrs Munn became her normal self again.

We chatted for half an hour or so. As a doctor I am glad to relate the worst of the influenza crisis had passed and the plucky invalid was indeed on the mend. Her chest was still wheezy and giving her problems and she was too weak to get out of bed, but given a week or so, I felt sure she would be up and about, and able to embrace her old routine.

'Dear old Albion,' she chuckled, patting the eiderdown. 'You know Doctor Watson, when I was very sick he visited me and jumped on the bed and rested his paws on my coverlet.'

'Albion is your dog, I take it,' said I, sampling a biscuit from the tin.

'He is a cross between a Newfoundland and a retriever, fur as black as pitch. Dogs are such devoted animals, they rarely desert you.'

'But they require a good deal of care,' murmured my companion thoughtfully. 'A Newfoundland is a large dog and must be fed his meat. I suppose a mix of bonemeal in a bowl suffices?'

'What on earth are you talking about?' laughed Mrs Munn.

'Nutrition,' said I, joining in. 'What Holmes is implying is that a large dog must be expensive to maintain.'

'Nonsense, my Albion has been dead these last eight years. A bowl of food would be next to useless and ignored. He is a spirit dog.'

'A ghost?'

'Certainly. Like I says, he came back to comfort me when I was very ill. Nearer to thee oh Lord.'

I confess that at this juncture I had heard enough to make me wonder if Mrs Munn had been susceptible to hallucinations. This would not have been unusual in such a case when a patient is delirious and in a high state of fever. In my own mind at least, the dog Albion she talked of was most likely imagined. The notion that her beloved pet had returned from the grave to visit her was clearly preposterous.

Before we left to catch our train she hugged us both and we promised to visit again soon.

The following morning at Baker Street we were enjoying an after-breakfast pipe, sat in our armchairs either side of the hearth and perusing the morning edition, Holmes the obituary column in particular, when there was a brisk knock at the door and Mrs Hudson entered our rooms accompanied by a tall, flaxen-haired individual with a notebook. He appeared wan and exhausted, not at peace with either himself or the world in general. I got up to pour him a cup of strong coffee for the fellow was in need of an honest stimulant.

'You were called out early, Gregson,' remarked Holmes, intently studying the detective, one of Scotland Yard's finest. 'That much is obvious, given your unshaven appearance and the singular fact you are still wearing your striped pyjama bottoms under your trousers.'

The inspector managed a weak smile. 'What a morning I've had, Mr Holmes. Not one but three burglaries along Ealing Broadway. The manager at the pawn shop and the two jewellers at Clarke's and Beresford's are beside themselves. They blame the lack of constables on duty, a non-existent night patrol. All nonsense, of course.'

'The amount stolen?'

'A considerable haul of cash, and gold and silver rings, watches and necklaces.'

'Chubb?'

'Chubb locks, yes. All the safes were of the American

type, compounded steel and a modern combination lock.'

'Lock-picks, the indispensable stethoscope and explosives,' I reflected.

Holmes frowned intently, 'A professional! An expert cracksman capable of pulling off "the treble". Was there much blast damage?'

'Minimal. Just the precise amount of explosive applied to the safes, the doors blown off their hinges with the result that there was little damage, and neighbours along Ealing Broadway heard nothing.'

'Who the devil would be capable of achieving the treble? Archie Burns of Millwall, certainly. Shem Vokins is also a contender, but Vokins is serving a lengthy stretch behind bars, is he not?'

'Vokins has served his time, Mr Holmes. He was released last month. I have it on good authority that he's recently moved from his old patch in Peckham, where he was living in digs. Archie Burns is dead. Spent his last night on earth drinking at the Queen Vic before being stabbed by a woman of ill repute and left for dead in the gutter. His funeral in the East End was well attended.'

'Well, Gregson, Shem's your most likely candidate, unless it's a northerner of course.'

'But he's vanished off the face of the earth, Mr Holmes.'

'A trifle overstated if I may say so, Gregson. Allow myself and Doctor Watson to make discreet enquiries on your behalf. Go to your bed, man, you looked fagged out. I shall send a telegram if we make any useful headway.'

* * *

That same morning a meeting was hastily convened with the Governor of Parkhurst Prison, Mr Alistair Monkton. Holmes and myself had visited the prison on many previous occasions. We were shown by the warder to Mr Monkton's office, an oak-panelled room the walls of which were adorned with photographs revealing his sporting prowess, for he had played both rugby and cricket at the higher level. The last Governor, Sir Philip Marsh, he of the yellow cadaverous face and stiff upper lip, was not popular and rarely discussed prisoners' details with outsiders. But Alistair was a younger fellow and more amenable. Holmes got on well with him and we were made very welcome, and served coffee.

'Please take a seat, gentlemen. Cigar?'

I was pleased to accept a Corona from the box, and snipped off the end, savouring the fine tobacco. Holmes did likewise.

'Shem Vokins was detained at Her Majesty's pleasure, I believe for ten years on account of a house break-in Kensington way.'

'Correct. He was a generally well-behaved prisoner, very polite, normally a fairly placid sort of individual. But there was a darker side. He had a reputation for knocking women about and on occasions could behave very violently for the most stupid, insignificant reasons.'

'Two distinct natures.'

'A dual personality, yes, but Vokins for most of the time was an ideal prisoner and we had no trouble. He served his time industriously.'

'The laundry?' asked Holmes, puffing on his cigar luxuriously.

'No.'

'The prison library?'

'Not a conscientious bookworm, no. He never once caught religion, either.'

'I must inform you Mr Monkton that Shem Vokins may have returned to his old habits. There was a treble robbery along Ealing Broadway last night, three safe's blown.'

'Have you any incriminating evidence?'

'I confess I am acting primarily on my own convictions. I believe that Shem Vokins is the only professional cracksman working in London capable of such a feat.'

'Well, after you've finished your coffee gentlemen I should very much like to take you outside to visit the prison yard, for I have something of outstanding interest to show you.'

At Parkhurst, as the reader will be aware, there is an area set aside for the gallows shed. Once hanged, the dead inmate is normally buried under quicklime. The gallows shed itself is an innocuous looking building stood on wooden stilts. There is room for all the usual apparatus of hanging, and enough space for the chaplain and other officials to oversee proceedings.

However, on this occasion we were not about to receive a guided tour of that infamous machinery of death, rather we were led round the side.

'Behold,' said the Governor, beaming with pleasure.

The long flower bed, with of its host of pansies and colourful perennials in bloom, with a mass of sunflowers growing by the wall, was truly striking. A little less well tended was the vegetable patch.

Nearby grew a selection of young apple and pear trees.

'All his own labour. We were astonished by Vokins' application to the task of brightening up the yard.'

'The close proximity of the gallows shed is a trifle off-putting,' remarked Holmes. 'I trust the gardens are closed to members of the public whenever there's a hanging?'

'Very droll,' laughed Mr Monkton, 'but you must admit, Mr Vokins possessed extremely green fingers.'

'The flower bed is most impressive,' I agreed, as we strolled back to the Governor's office, wondering at that brief flowering oasis amongst the grim prison surroundings.

By late afternoon we were in Ealing Broadway, walking briskly along the High Street. Holmes suddenly seized my elbow and hustled me through the door to an ironmonger, Carson & Co.

'My dear boy,' said Holmes, hurrying across to the counter, where a young lad in a brown work coat was busily employed filling a box with candles. 'I require packets of seeds, a spade, a hoe, a decent fork.'

'You're interested in taking up gardening.'

'You're most perceptive. I am but an amateur.'

'All gardeners are amateurs, sir. There's always something new to learn. That's the glory of it. I can supply all your needs. We have a new line in garden tools and a selection of seed packets over on the rack.'

'Perhaps I might be persuaded to purchase various grades of terracotta flower pots.'

'We had a gentleman in on Tuesday like you, sir. But lore he was fussy. Got what he wanted though, more than an hour he spent in the shop.'

'What did he purchase?' said I, feigning interest.

'See them lovely gleaming, freshly-oiled spades and the brand-new forks and rakes? He had one of them each, box-loads of seeds, a watering can, even an enamel mug and plate. Gave me a five-guinea bank note, he did.'

'I know who that is,' said my companion, studying the labels on the seed packets. 'Silas, the old local with the leg brace, swears he was at Waterloo. How he gets about fails me, let alone keep that garden of his in such fine fettle.'

'Mr Silas,' muttered the counter boy, making a point of frowning and forgetting his candles.

'Come now, you know of whom I speak, the fellow who dresses like a navvy, ties string round his gaiters.'

'A bit withdrawn and morose'.

'Somewhat of an australopithecine, certainly. I presume all the tools and seeds and so forth were delivered to his home address? Such a large order.'

'Told me he'd just moved on to an allotment. Got his own little shed, stove, garden bench, very comfy. Nice paraffin lamp.'

'Which allotment?'

'The Borough allotments, sir. They're behind the recreational ground, five minutes from the Underground. Lots of locals have a plot over there. Are you paying cash, sir? For all your goods, I mean. I'll gather 'em up and wrap 'em while you're stood here, if you like.'

'I think I'd prefer to return tomorrow morning

if you don't mind. Thank you all the same. Good day.'

We hurried in the direction of the Borough park. Was this keen customer the young lad told us of really Shem Vokins? My friend remained cautious.

'I should not wish to alert Mr Vokins, the allotment-holder, just yet. Let him rake his patch in peace for now. We shall search him out later this evening when the light starts to fade.'

'Could he be armed?' I asked.

'Hard to say, Watson. You have your service revolver handy?'

'Indeed'.

'Well, that offers us a modicum of protection at least. You will recall the Governor mentioning his peccadillo for beating up young ladies of the night. A violent streak such as that is far from healthy in the human psyche. I should say Vokins would be volatile and problematic if cornered. The mention of the allotment shed interests me.'

'Oh, those!' I laughed. 'My dear Holmes, they are usually nothing more than flimsy shacks tacked together from bits of plyboard, planks of wood and a roll of asphalt. If you sneeze too hard they most likely fall down.'

'Not all allotment sheds are quite so derisible, Watson. I recall a most sturdy construction upon an allotment in Thornton Heath. Why, one could almost live in such a place during the warmer months of the year.'

'Perhaps that is Shem Vokins's intention. To lie low and escape the attention of the police. Why, the stolen valuables could easily be secreted amongst the flower pots.'

'Quite, dear boy. Have you a cigarette? My most pressing concern is to telegraph Gregson and inform him of our movements. After we have visited Ealing post office let us while away an hour or two at the tea rooms. I should quite fancy an omelette for I am absolutely famished.'

As the shadows of evening fell, we made our way to the recreation ground. The place was for the most part deserted, save for a nanny pushing a spindly pram and some children aimlessly kicking a football. We wandered past a drinking fountain to the railings on the far side. A gap existed in the park fence that led straight on to the path. There was roughly an acre of allotments spread across the land. The weather had been warm and sunny and most of those intent on a few hours watering and pruning, else relaxing with a mug of tea in one of the innumerable huts thereabouts, enjoying the splendid sunset over Ealing, were on their way home. This made the job of locating Shem Vokins that much easier. I saw many a nut-brown face. These men of suburbia in their flat tweed caps, old baggy seconds and hefty mud-caked hobnail boots bade us 'good evening' and went upon their way. One by one the oil lamps about the allotment were extinguished. Falling-apart wooden sheds, shanties and huts of corrugated iron gradually became dark and deserted as each owner abandoned his smallholding.

All except one, on the far side. Holmes paid particular attention to the wavering flame from a solitary lamp placed in the window. The pathway was either bordered with old railway sleepers or clay bricks. By now the temperature was becoming chill, the darkness starting to encroach on the allotment, making everything shadowy and indistinct. All except the hut with the lamp.

'Come Watson, Gregson and his compatriots will be with us on the hour, for now it is two against one.'

We approached the shed warily. I observed the usual water-butt, a heap of horse manure, and the glint of a brand-new watering can, as yet undented and showing no sign of mould or rust on its shiny enamel surface. A solitary spade, half dug into the ground, was wedged amongst the broad beans. Wasting no time, my colleague called out.

'Shem! Have you boiled some water in the kettle, I'd quite fancy a mug of tea so we can discuss the robberies along Ealing Broadway. Three safes blown in, which represents something of a record, surely. It takes a first rate cracksman to complete the treble, a safe blower of singular talent.'

'Go away, I'm a-warning you. If you value your life, scram.'

'You are armed.'

'Nah'.

'Then pour me a mug of tea and come outside where I can see you better.'

'Who are you, the police?'

'I'm a consulting detective.'

'Go to hell.'

'I believe I know where the stolen valuables are stashed.'

'Go on'.

'Your shiny new spade dug in amongst the broad beans indicates where the treasure lies buried, does it not?'

'I'm not saying. Now clear off, I'm losing my patience and there's no telling what I'm capable of once the crimson mist descends upon me.'

'You've been busy digging that spot for quite a while'

'I'm warning you.'

'The police will be here shortly, and I am not alone.'

'I saw both of you clumsy oafs over by the park railings ages ago, but I tell you what, I'm not going back.'

'Not going back where?'

'The prison. I already done a ten-year stretch and that's enough.'

We heard movement in the shed, the sound of heavy boots on flimsy floorboards, the sagging and the creaking of rotten wood. He was getting restless, clumping around feeling like a cooped-up rat in a cage. But anything, I imagined, was better than sharing a cell at Parkhurst, and he would not compromise his new-found freedom for anything, which made him doubly dangerous. He said he was unarmed, that he carried no weapon, but I was not so sure. Holmes got up and calmly walked across to the shiny new spade. I covered him with my service revolver, ready to smash the oil lantern if necessary.

'Go on, sir,' a voice goaded, 'if you want the stolen loot you'll have to dig first.'

'I fully intend to,' said Holmes, taking off his overcoat and rolling up his sleeves. He was doing his best to act as bait and tempt Vokins out of the shed into the open, for while he remained inside he was an unknown quantity.

As he was about to grip the spade by the handle, Holmes suddenly froze. He did not move a muscle, for out of nowhere came a large black dog, a giant, that bounded across the bean patch and launched itself at my shocked companion, its green eyes flashing like emeralds piercing the darkness.

Losing his footing, Holmes tumbled backwards and fell into the stinking pile of manure. There was a good deal of laughter as Inspector Gregson and his Scotland Yard force marched towards the shed. But the laughter soon turned to incredulous horror when one of the officers discovered an almost invisible trip-wire, leading from the base of the spade's haft to a thin metal contact plate positioned just below the surface of the soil. If Holmes had struck the spade with his foot, as all of us are wont to do when forcibly digging a patch of ground, this would have triggered an explosion of some force, for buried beneath the broad beans were not only the stolen valuables from the pawnbrokers and the jewellers, but a rigged bomb device primed to detonate at the slightest vibration.

Holmes had been very lucky, and to think we had that menacing black hound to thank for saving our lives, though where the dog had come from or where it had gone was anybody's guess.

Shem Vokins never did return to prison for it was later discovered he had slit his own throat from ear to ear with a razor during the commotion and, until police officers appeared with a stretcher, lay stiff and dead upon the sagging, rotten floorboards of the allotment shed.

6

The Bundle of Sticks

In the autumn of 1901, the year of our beloved Queen's death that heralded the inevitable passing of an age, I was sat at the table before breakfast reading a copy of *The Lancet*. Holmes had gone out early on one of his cases and was not due back for a while, and at that moment a lady of middle years breezed into our rooms, depositing her brolly and handbag on the couch.

'So, who are we this morning?' said I, hardly bothering to look up. 'Miss Parsons, the insufferable old spinster from Balham or Miss Cleaver, the old washerwoman from Crouch End?'

I patiently waited for Holmes to emerge from his masterly disguise, like a phoenix rising from the ashes. It was not to be.

'I am Miss Fowler Tutt and I am Head Librarian at Marylebone Public Library,' said she, with more than a hint of disdain in her voice. 'Is Mr Holmes about? You, I take it, must be Doctor Watson.'

'My apologies,' I blustered, and began babbling banalities about how overcast the weather had been of late, and how awful the state of traffic along Marylebone Road. I offered her a cup of coffee from the pot, which she accepted, and was about to inform her that my colleague was not expected for another half hour when, to my surprise, the door burst open and a haughty lady, tall in stature, coiffured to perfection, her make-up exactingly applied, her dress sense immaculate, walked gracefully across to the mantelpiece, plucked a pipe from the rack and began filling it with tobacco.

'Halloa! You've come about the murder of Sir Hugh Zaron found stabbed to death on the steps of the Natural History Museum, I take it? A dismal business, and I agree with you there is a Roman connection.'

'My dear sir, how on earth...?'

'A trifling observation. You are, madam, carrying beneath your arm a treasured copy of Shakespeare's *Julius Caesar*. Like me, you have every reason to suspect the curator's murder bears striking similarities to the scene where Caesar struggles to escape as the conspirators close in upon him near Pompey's statue and hack him to death. "Et tu Bruté? Then fall Caesar". Act three, scene one.'

'You amaze me! I was commuting to work by train and spent some time reading a newspaper account of the murder, quickly forming the impression of a Roman connection certainly, but furthermore...'

'A bundle of sticks was left at the scene of the crime.'

'A bundle of sticks?' said I, somewhat dismissive.

'To be more precise, a bundle of birch rods – the symbol of magisterial power in ancient Rome. Incredibly, Watson, there is listed a "Bundle of Sticks Society". I took the liberty to call on one of Mycroft's acquaintances at the Diogenes Club, a certain

Professor Saunders who works as a manuscript-keeper at the British Museum Library and has compiled a voluminous catalogue of secret societies. He is an acknowledged expert on the Society's code of conduct and I asked him to clear up certain points. Evidently, to break a sacred oath could result in dismissal, confiscation of regalia, else a substantial fine.'

'And more serious malpractice?' I enquired.

'Termination. Although there is no real evidence. The Society could, in theory, appoint a chosen and trusted acolyte to do away with the member. There should be no escape. I shall provide you with certain examples: breaching confidentiality – an exposé where the sacred practices and rituals of the society have been leaked to a national newspaper for financial gain; else direct disobedience to 'an oracle' contravening the laws and long-held beliefs of the society. In either case, the outcome would be extremely ruthless and unpleasant. That is the gist of Professor Saunders's findings,' said my colleague, considering his long cherry wood pipe.

'Goodness,' cried Miss Fowler Tutt, gathering her brolly and handbag and getting up to leave. 'Listening to these revelations I quite forgot the time. I am due in my office for a meeting of junior librarians.'

'One further point,' said Holmes. 'I am informed by Professor Saunders that the Bundle of Sticks Society meets in Bloomsbury on the fourth Thursday of every month.'

I had hardly finished shaving and was dressing in my bedroom when a constable of police called round and delivered to Mrs Hudson a sealed official envelope addressed to Holmes and bearing the stamp 'Mortuary, Police Division 60, Private & Confidential'.

'You will be aware, Watson,' said he, now looking more like the Holmes I knew and ripping open the envelope with a paper knife, 'that I have made it my business to nurture and befriend certain individuals of lowly employ inhabiting the area of the London mortuaries. Maurice Karavitz is just such a fellow. Realising the corpse of the murdered Sir Hugh Zaron was to be conveyed to the most convenient mortuary in the Kensington precinct I immediately wired Mr Karavitz and am now able to ascertain from him certain forensic details otherwise unavailable. He is of course an elderly, deaf attendant who haunts such places of autopsy and will assist the police surgeon by the subsequent removal of the body to the iced storage room on a wheeled gurney. Now let us read the results.'

The briefing on official paper ran to a couple of pages, which included crude pencil sketches and diagrams.

Dear Mr Holmes, thank you for your enquiry. Once the police surgeon had departed I lifted the rubber sheet as you directed and formed my own analysis. I took special note of the wounds and the trajectory of the blade. Varying depths, different angles, altogether wounds to the nape of the neck, shoulder blades, lower spine, one or two defensive scars to the palms of hands, two digits cut through to the gristle (see sketch). In my opinion, sir, a vicious premeditated attack by an unknown group of individuals.

To conclude, the specimen was stabbed in the back. I have never in my entire career as a mortuary attendant seen anything quite like it. A perforated aorta of the heart was the cause of death.

I am, sir

Your obedient servant,

Maurice

That evening Miss Fowler Tutt returned to our lodgings and shared with us a modest supper of curried chicken, one of Mrs Hudson's specialities, and one of Holmes's personal favourites.

I observed that Miss Fowler Tutt had brought with her an old book, a calf-bound volume that looked as if it had been dredged out of the Thames. The tooled leather binding was green with damp and mottled with stains, many of its pages stuck together, and the spine requiring gluing.

After supper she sat on the sofa and, while Holmes and myself lit our pipes, prepared to discuss her latest research concerning the murder of Sir Hugh Zaron. She had earlier visited the lower basement of Marylebone Public Library. Not normally open to members of the public, here were stored many old books, some of them very rare, damaged by fire and flooding and awaiting the attention of the conservator. The basement was out of bounds to all except senior staff and had remained sealed for many years. Miss Fowler Tutt made a discovery that was to prove crucial to our understanding of the Bundle of Sticks Society, for the old book she had brought to show us, long out of print, gave a concise history of that secretive organisation.

The Society was originally founded by a Doctor Poole in 1768. Upon his death at the age of eighty, he was embalmed in tar, save for the head, and in this preserved state presented to the Natural History museum by his wife and surviving son as a gift for perpetuity. The specimen was deemed undesirable by the staff and members of the museum board but a bargain was struck and for a considerable bequest to the Department of Geology, Dr Poole's embalmed corpse was removed to a suitable place of storage downstairs amongst the dried out, dusty old examples of taxidermy, the crocodiles, alligators and similarly embalmed reptiles, rare species of lizard, gecko and so forth.

The tarry, mummified remains of Doctor Poole, with its by now shrunken, hairless head, thus remained long forgotten and neglected in this section for many years.

'Mr Holmes, on impulse I could not resist a journey upon the subterranean railway to South Kensington to enquire as to the whereabouts of this historic specimen embalmed in tar and labelled "Dr Poole".'

'Ha, bravo Miss Fowler Tutt, I take my hat off to you. And the department was forthcoming?'

'Indeed, they fully co-operated. A Mr Packham recalled as a student venturing downstairs to the preserved reptile section and for the first time gazing upon the crisply embalmed old curiosity when it was pointed out to him. Alas, he explained the ancient relic had gone missing from the store some time ago. He mentioned that no other person in living memory, apart from myself, had enquired after it, save for the previous curator, the late Sir Hugh Zaron. Mr Packham went on to say it was common knowledge that Sir Hugh had barely finished writing a manuscript for a proposed book that documented the life and teachings of the antiquarian Dr Poole, revealing certain controversial aspects of the Bundle of Sticks Society, which he helped found. The book was to be published by Blackwoods and the manuscript due to be delivered when Sir Hugh was stabbed to death on the steps of the museum. *The Daily Telegraph* was to publish extracts. Mr Holmes, what if this secret society was about to be exposed, a scandal of some kind?'

'Quite likely,' acknowledged my companion, puffing thoughtfully on his pipe. 'Sir Hugh may even have been a member of the Society himself. We can only conjecture.'

It was with great sorrow that the following morning my companion learned of the death of Mycroft's old friend and fellow member of the Diogenes Club, Professor Saunders, M.A. M. Lit, the keeper of manuscripts at the British Museum Library, who was found stricken by apoplexy while seated at his desk, writing letters. Strangest of all, a presence of pitch was reported adhered to the ivory door knob and blotches of embedded tar were found in the fibres of the Wilton carpet, impossible to wash out with any amount of soapy water. Scotland Yard insisted no foul play was suspected and that Saunders had most likely died from natural causes.

My friend was sat in his armchair pondering the suspicious circumstances surrounding the manuscript-keeper's sudden death, when a runner from the British Museum Library delivered into our possession a tiny manila envelope entrusted to the messenger by a member of staff loyal to the late professor. Inside was an ominous note.

> Beware the Oracle. They meet at No. 19 Bedford Square at 9 o'clock. They plan an outrage at our dear departed Queen's funeral at Windsor. For God's sake act Holmes. They have found me out. Dress in black robes like monks. The password is 'Hail the Oracle' at the door.

In due haste it was arranged that Miss Fowler Tutt should stitch together out of old coats a selection of monks' robes, the various cloth dyed black in accordance with the Society's regalia and dress code. At half past eight we should meet up and henceforth take a cab to Bedford Square. The Bundle of Sticks Society evidently held its meetings at a fashionable white stuccoed Georgian house, the square being populated by wealthy persons of rank and title.

Holmes's plan was that the three of us should infiltrate their number. The demise of Professor Saunders seemed to spur him on. The traces of tar found at the scene remained a puzzling mystery yet to be properly explained.

'We must carry a weapon, my dear Watson. I'll

wager there's some hefty ruffians amongst the acolytes.'

'What if they decide to search us at the door?' said I, pouring us each a glass of whiskey. There appeared to be few options. My service revolver was far too bulky and would be difficult to conceal. Neither of us had much use for knives but Holmes soon came up with a viable alternative – a weapon that could be easily hidden upon his person and yet prove highly effective when required.

'Now, where's that short blowpipe, the longer ones are much too unwieldy. They used to hang either side of the mantelpiece. The poisonous quill darts I know for certain are kept in my watercolour paint box in the cupboard.'

My companion dashed into his bedroom, knelt down and rummaged beneath the bed for his rare collection of primitive weapons which, if memory serves me correctly, were a gift from the King of Nepal for services rendered. They used to hang in our front room. Their whereabouts were a complete mystery. I wondered if Mrs Hudson had turfed them out when she last tidied up.

'Holmes!' I shouted from my armchair. 'Didn't Mrs Hudson get rid of them?' I prepared to light my pipe. 'I seem to remember a load of your chemistry pipettes and glass test tubes went the way of the refuse collector. You know, when she last had that clear out when we returned from a concert to find the furniture rearranged and my clothes lying on the floor.'

'By Jove, I've found it, Watson!' he shouted back. 'You know, the bamboo's not even cracked. I'd better put in a bit of practice. How long before we leave for Bedford Square?'

'Miss Fowler Tutt is arriving at half eight,' said I, puffing on my briar.

'Once you learn how to purse the lower lip properly, the rest follows naturally. You must exhale a deep breath from the diaphragm and force the air out from the lungs. After all, I'm not perfecting the art of killing monkeys high up in the tree canopy, rather stunning an adversary. I shall be using the number twos, a mild poison-tipped dart.'

'Perfectly proper,' said I.

'My dear fellow, as uninvited guests it is imperative our faces be hidden from view. The cowled hoods of the monks' robes must be drawn over our heads and we mustn't forget the all important password, "Hail the Oracle".'

That night the fog descended over London, the foul pollution of coal fires and industrial smoke combining to create the dreaded 'pea souper' so hated by the populace both east and west of the Thames. I recall the funeral of Queen Victoria was due to take place the next day, the streets of the city being prepared for that most solemn of occasions. Her request had been for a white draped gun carriage and no use of black, a significant change in mourning etiquette for the time. Like most Londoners, both myself and Sherlock Holmes ordinarily wore black arm bands in respect of our great monarch's passing.

Our hansom rattled through Bloomsbury and past

the British Museum, its shadowy façade dimly visible through the fog, the glow from street lamps indistinct and hazy. We must have seemed an incongruous sight, the three of us dressed in monks' robes. The cabman I was sure took us for some dour religious order from the Outer Hebrides come down to London for the funeral.

Upon entering Bedford Square, I saw at No. 19 a crowd of black-robed monks already mounting the flight of steps, else murmuring to one another beneath the columned portico.

We paid the cabman his fare and joined the queue forming to go inside. The lanterns above the grand porch cast a chilly light, with most, like us, wanting to reach the warmth of the fine Regency house to escape the cloying chilly vapour blanketing the square. At the door we were asked the password as a mere formality, and stepped inside the lighted entrance hall with its parquet floor and busts of Roman emperors in various niches. There was a nude statue of a warrior on a plinth, fine frescoes and a marble staircase. It was like being in a palace. I was quite overwhelmed by the opulence, the splendour of the décor. A string quartet was playing Vivaldi. We were guided to a room known as 'The Temple'. All were wearing their hoods so none could be identified. For all I knew there might be cabinet ministers, lords and grand dukes amongst them.

There was a suitably Corinthian feel to the architecture of the place. With the exception of Holmes, we sat in rows beneath a beautifully painted ceiling depicting the Labours of Hercules. A large satin-covered cabinet with a curtained opening at the front was placed to one side of a raised dais, a lectern on the other.

'Where's the Oracle?' I wondered out loud, searching the room for a golden calf or the bronze head of a bull.

'The Oracle can be a person,' Miss Fowler Tutt whispered in my ear, anxious not to be overheard. 'Not necessarily an inanimate object like the statue of a goddess, Doctor Watson.'

Still, I was somewhat disappointed not to be focusing upon some graven image, for I was convinced an idol of some sort would be essential to the ceremony. Holmes, I noticed with some amusement, was stood with his bamboo blowpipe at the ready, just behind a pillar, everybody's attention being the other way, for a chief acolyte had just approached the lectern.

'Good evening, everyone,' he said, in a friendly way. 'Hail the Oracle.'

'Hail the Oracle!' we all of us repeated, a wave of applause rippling round The Temple. The hairs on the nape of my neck bristled for the expectant atmosphere was electric. The gas jets dimmed although the raised dais remained bathed in a soft, tranquil glow.

'Hail Dr Poole.'

A gurney was wheeled out of the satin cabinet by two acolytes. On it was a corpse embalmed in tar, save for the hairless head whose horridly glazed eyes stared unseeing up at the elaborately painted ceiling. All was hushed now, no one uttered a sound, but bowed respectfully. We did likewise, following the herd. The mummified body was swiftly wheeled back inside the cabinet, the curtains swished across the entrance and there followed a brief interlude.

The suspense was tangible. The pregnant pause in the proceedings did not last long, however, for the curtains flapped open again and from the satin cabinet a ragged, crinkly figure stumped awkwardly over to the lectern, leaving a trail of tar in its wake. The pitch-black thing waited for the raucous applause to die down before speaking to the assembled gathering.

'My friends!' It spoke in a croaky, glutinous way. 'For so many winters and summers I have slept in my cocoon of tar, until now. At last free from the restraints of the underworld, I can join you to share our greatest triumph – the establishment of a true Senate, with my fondest admirer, Mr Lardsby, installed in Westminster as the new Caesar. The Emperor of all Britain – England, Scotland, Ireland and Wales. For the first time in many a long century the *fasces* shall once more be held aloft!'

The room went berserk, the noise of shouting and wild applause was deafening. Did these poor, deluded fools really believe this sham, this utter tosh, I wondered incredulously. It was then I noticed out of the corner of my eye that Holmes, still concealed behind his pillar, had raised his blowpipe to his mouth. He was poised to fire a dart, lining up a shot. Suddenly, *pithzzzz*, I heard a sharp outtake of breath. The tar thing meanwhile raised up one of its black, encrusted paws and commanded silence.

'Tomorrow.'

The dart struck home and the tar man, the imposter masquerading as Doctor Poole, brushed his forehead, temporarily distracted by what must have felt like a bee sting to him. 'The end of a tiresome line of kings and queens, no more Henrys, no more Edwards, no more Elizabeths, no more Georges, no...'

Members of the Society, emboldened by his inflammatory remarks, drank in every word of the anarchist's speech. This was what they wanted to hear. More about the dissolution of the monarchy, although his delivery had started to falter. Miss Fowler Tutt seized my arm and whispered so that none around us could hear.

'Doctor Watson, he forgets what to say, he's confused.'

'I – we – the Queen's gun carriage, a limpet bomb. You – we shall – they – I – we are all...'

Before he could make a total ass of himself, the pair of acolytes who had been stood to one side of the dais acted decisively and led the faint and stumbling 'Dr Poole' back into his satin cabinet. I heard raised voices and there was a good deal of commotion.

Although the reborn man of tar had been unable to complete his 'call to arms' speech, the general mood inside The Temple was still boisterous and, following a delay of five minutes, the throng were privileged once more to witness the gurney being wheeled out, the rigid mummified corpse reclining on top.

The audience of hardened anarchists rose to their feet and the preserved corpse received a standing ovation.

The gas jets slowly came up, and people started to file out.

Meanwhile, outside in Bedford Square, preparations were underway for an unprecedented police operation. While the meeting had been taking place, a convoy of thirty Black Marias had queued along the street. The square had been evacuated, the residents having been told to find somewhere else for the night, and sealed off. Eight divisions of police conscripted from all over the capital were gathered in the thick fog. Armed officers and ferocious bull terriers, police attack dogs specially brought in with their handlers from the compound at Kennington, were amassed at the rear of the property, and as the first group of sinister robed figures emerged from the Georgian mansion they were immediately placed under arrest.

'Lardsby should have suffered temporary blindness for twenty minutes or so. Paralysis of the lower extremities, a stiff neck, an inability to swallow,' remarked my erstwhile colleague at breakfast, attacking his ham and egg with a fulsome appetite. 'Now, a number four should have stunned an elephant and a number six killed him outright.'

'The heat resistant rubber suit and gauze head mask were worn to great effect, I thought, creating the illusion of being embalmed in tar.'

'Indeed my dear fellow, Lardsby would have donned the same hideous apparel when he breached the British Museum Library and entered Professor Saunders' office uninvited, spreading a form of pitch, else tradesman's thick black gloss paint, on the carpet and door handle, causing the poor fellow to die of shock.'

'Will he hang?'

'Undoubtedly, but for the crime of treason, of course. As will certain other anarchists rounded up that night.'

'When did you decide to brief Scotland Yard and talk to the Minister?'

'My mind was made up, thanks to Miss Fowler Tutt's most revealing lunchtime foray to Kensington, where she discovered the embalmed corpse of Doctor Poole was missing. I speculated that Sir Hugh was determined to destroy the Society for he had found out about a certain serious threat against the national interest. Now we learn there was a dastardly anarchic plot to bomb Queen Victoria's funeral cortège at Windsor, to kill the King and many foreign dignitaries and royal personages.'

'Well, thank God the funeral passed without incident. Our dear departed Queen now rests in eternal peace beside her beloved Albert at the Mausoleum at Frogmore.'

'You know, Watson, my intuition tells me that our librarian friend Miss Fowler Tutt may yet appear in the New Year Honours List. Mycroft assures me that her significant contribution to the downfall of Lardsby and his cohorts has been recognised in high places.'

7

The Chance Encounter

One morning I emerged into our untidy sitting room to find my fellow lodger, Mr Sherlock Holmes, sat bolt upright at his cluttered desk, wearing his old dressing gown and totally engrossed in reading an officially headed letter. The remains of a still-smouldering cigarette was held precariously betwixt the long bony fingers of his left hand, allowing stray ash to be deposited into a beaker of murky alkaline solution, for he had, until the morning post arrived, been busy at his chemistry.

There clung to the room still an awful, pervading stench of some invisible vapour that both irritated my eyes and caused my nose to tingle uncomfortably.

'Any news from Mycroft?' said I, coughing and heading for the breakfast table and the covered heated dishes laid out so fastidiously by Mrs Hudson.

'No, no, our correspondent is none other than Doctor Proust. You recall, my dear Watson, we dined with him at his house. I think it was concerning Bankcroft, the child poisoner.'

'Ah, at the prison. I remember Felix Proust. It was shortly before the hanging at Exeter. He is a genuinely caring physician and a pioneer in the field of assessing the criminally insane. He kept jars of their dissected brains in his study.'

'Be that as it may, he is now the head of department at the Garland, a private residence in St John's Wood, utilised for the long-term care of those afflicted by nervous disorders, and in charge of a ward. Before you tuck into your ham and eggs, my dear fellow, take a read of it, will you?'

Holmes passed me the letter. I propped it against the toast rack and poured myself a cup of coffee.

My Dear Holmes,
So glad to learn from Inspector Gregson that all is well with you and that you are busy and productive, and still living at Baker Street. Since my prison days I have taken on more and more cases of a less criminal nature, my specialist studies being confined to psychoanalysis. I have been offered a post at the Garland in St John's Wood, which I have accepted.

I am writing to you on account of a patient recently admitted to my ward by the name of Brocklehurst. Yes, he is one of the Brocks of Fenhurst Place, Westdene, the family who for generations have owned all that land and estates in Sussex. The father, old Archie Segram, recently passed away and being a widower my patient's brother Edward, the elder son, will inherit the title. Peregrine Brocklehurst himself is in Ward 3. An earnest young man of a shy and retiring disposition, he recently suffered a shock of nerves that has left his mind quite unhinged. He normally works in the City and has a modern bachelor flat in Dolphin Square. I should say he is a classic psychotic delusional case, but his story is quite fascinating, indeed exceptional, and will appeal to you. Please come at once.

Yours,
Felix

Holmes could not resist the lure of the unusual, so after breakfast we took a cab to St John's Wood. The private hospital was in a smart residential district, situated discreetly in a large semi-detached Italianate villa in a quiet, leafy street. In no time we were sat around a table in Doctor Proust's consulting room with the aforementioned patient.

The poor fellow looked washed out, all in, he had not shaved for days and his hair was tousled and unkempt. He was sorely in need of a barber. His well-tailored clothes were rumpled, his dirty shirt collar askew and not properly studded. He possessed a curious habit of staring continually into space, his mouth hanging open, the protruding lower lip pouting like a belligerent trout hovering amongst the reed beds of a stream. He was, I should judge, five and twenty years of age and at first seemed rigid and uncooperative.

'Come, Brocklehurst, no need to be over reticent. These fellows are trustworthy and well known to me. Explain your experience of last weekend.'

'I met a woman on the platform of Victoria Station,' he said at length. 'A young lady by the name of Miss Hardwicke. She had just come off the boat train and was, like me, travelling on to Brighton by the Pullman service. She was very beautiful, a lady of impeccable character, a wonderful pure soul, an angel of such...'

Proust held up his hand and stopped proceedings with a wag of his finger.

'Try and avoid hysterics, don't be so dramatic, Brocklehurst. Pray continue, but keep your account always simple and to the point.'

'Very well,' said he, totally unphased by the doctor's stern direction. 'For the entire journey Miss Hardwicke sat opposite me in the compartment. I took out my pipe for a while and smoked. I could not take my eyes off her. I adored her from the first and I honestly believe she was likewise attracted. We talked and laughed a lot. She found me amusing and I found her a wonderful listener, always attentive, always prepared to smile at my silly jokes. I confess that by the time our train entered Balcombe tunnel I was enjoying her company like no other and as we drew into the terminus at Brighton I was a young man in love.'

'And what did you yearn to ask this Miss Hardwicke?' said Doctor Proust, shifting in his chair.

'I wanted to ask her hand in marriage. I wished to devote my life to her.'

'Was this not a trifle extreme? A train journey of an hour and a half or so and you wish to wed this woman? I should be tempted to categorise your behaviour as obsessional.'

'Not at all, Doctor Proust,' he reasoned. 'I did not mean to infer I was about to drop down on my knees like a besotted fool outside W.H. Smith's kiosk, I merely intended to invite Miss Hardwicke to tea at the Metropole, perhaps to share a ride on

Herr Volks's new electric railway up to Black Rock. She had at this time in her possession a weighty canvas travelling bag and her parasol, for you will recall she had only just returned from France on the boat train – Paris, in fact. I would have liked to have assisted her with her baggage, at least to the cab rank, and shared addresses.'

'But this was not to be?'

'Unfortunately no, for in the short time we had I seemed unable to fully express my feelings and put into words what I knew in my heart to be profoundly true, that I loved her. Before I knew it she was dashing off into the crowd, waving goodbye.'

'But all was not entirely lost...' said Proust, glancing at his case notes.

'Thank goodness that before parting she, in the sweetest way, pecked me on the cheek, and asked if I might, as a small favour on my way to Seaford via the branch, mind stopping off at Tide Mills Halt, simply to convey a brief message to her uncle, a Mister Eaves, who was the Station Master, that she had returned home from France and was setting her life to order. This of course offered me the perfect opportunity to find out exactly where she lived.'

'Did Miss Hardwicke possess any distinguishing marks, a mole, a scar, dimples?' enquired Holmes, seizing his briar pipe and sucking on the stem.

'In truth, sir, I cannot recall – even the colour of her eyes I am unsure of. Grey, blue, green, violet, yet she had copious blonde curls and wore a summery skirt and bonnet, and her perfect features even the gods of Olympus would applaud.'

'Quite so, pray do not keep us in suspense. Tide Mills, you say. Carry on!'

'My connecting train was waiting at Lewes. The coast stopping service passed through Newhaven where, as usual, I saw the many fishing vessels in port. I was well content to be back in this part of dear old Sussex, returning to my ancestral home at Westdene, a welcome respite from London and my hectic life as a City broker.

'At Tide Mills I alighted upon the timber platform and asked a member of staff, a senior porter manning the level-crossing gates, where I might find the Station Master, Mr Eaves. He politely informed me that the gentleman was presently having lunch and could be found at the railway house along the lane. The front door was normally open to visitors at this time of day, he confided.'

'Now,' said Doctor Proust seriously, shuffling his papers, 'we are on the precipice of what I should term as the first stage of your breakdown. I will in all honesty say to Mr Holmes and Doctor Watson that I diagnose here the beginnings of classic psychotic delusional behaviour. I shall for now leave my findings confidential. Pray continue Brocklehurst, if you please.'

'From the moment I entered the Station Master's house, I sensed something was wrong. I was somehow out of kilter with the prevailing sombre mood – my carefree, happy-go-lucky attitude was misplaced. "Mr Eaves?", I called from the rose-covered porch. "May I come in? I shall not take up too much of your time. I have a message for you." "Message!" a loud voice boomed. "They usually bell telegraph messages

112

along the wire." I heard footsteps and there, stood before me stroking his beard, was the Station Master. He was a great bear of a man dressed in his customary top hat and frock coat. He grinned, revealing a mouth full of blackened and yellowing crooked teeth. "Come into my parlour, you can explain yourself, young man, while I eat my cold beef sandwich."

'This I did, or at least attempted to do, for I was about to speak in the fondest terms of our chance encounter on Victoria Station, and the pleasant journey I had shared with Miss Hardwicke to Brighton on the Pullman and convey her good wishes, when I happened to observe with some abhorrence a portrait, a framed photograph wreathed in mourning crêpe, placed next to a vase of lilies upon the old pianola over by the window.

' "A message for you," I blurted out, my composure surely tested, my mind in a whirl, for I had just seen a memoriam photograph showing the face of Miss Hardwicke, whom I had barely met but a few hours previously. "A message from your niece."

' "Get out!" he raged, raising his great ham fist and threatening to knock me to the floor. "Shame on you sir, a gentleman an' all. My niece is *dead*. She fell from the cliffs but a day past, it was an accident. The funeral's to be held at Saint Leonard's Church in Seaford. Begone."

'I confess, as I hurried up the sunny lane towards the level crossing, all I could see in my mind's eye was my darling Miss Hardwicke cruelly reduced from a human form to a dreadful memoriam photograph atop an old dusty piano. Dead. How could she be dead? All the way back to Westdene I was consumed by a fever of anxiety.'

'Stop there, if you will, Brocklehurst. Let's share this pot of tea before it turns cold. Cream? Sugar? Help yourselves. Digestives, anyone?'

During this brief interlude, while we drank tea and smoked our pipes, the patient once more fell into a hopeless reverie, chewing his bottom lip all the while, no doubt dreaming of his lost love. Doctor Proust brought us all to order by tapping his teaspoon on the edge of the table.

'Brocklehurst? There's more to tell us, I believe?'

'Indeed,' he mumbled, taking a sip of tepid tea.

'Let's move on to the following day. It is a Sunday, at your golf club, Seaford Head golf links. The course is on the cliffs, you say here in my notes, very windy and a tough climb up a steep slope from the clubhouse. You had your five iron and had just reached the summit of the slope.'

'I and another member, Mister Hadley, who I often play with at weekends, were strolling across the links. It's all scrubland, rabbit warrens, tussocky grass up there. There is no fence and the edge of the cliff is close by. Glance over your shoulder and you can see the town, the wide sweep of the bay, Corsica Hall House, the Martello Tower. The way we were headed with our golf bags lies Cuckmere Haven. My home at Westdene is some way across the Downs. The manor house has been in our family for generations, since William the . . .'

'Come now, try to concentrate on your golfing,' said Doctor Proust good-naturedly, patting his patient on the shoulder by way of encouragement.

'Forgive me, the golf. Well, I had whacked the ball a fair distance, not a bad swing. By now, as often occurs at this time of year, the mist had drifted in off the sea, visibility was far from poor, but nonetheless areas of the course were becoming hazy and indistinct. The moist vapour was starting to affect my game. *Clop.* I struck another ball sixty yards or so and then we both noticed a young woman running frantically along the cliff path. She was wearing only a night shirt and I recall her poor little hands outstretched before her like tiny talons grasping at thin air, strands of her abundant hair blown about her face by the stiff inshore breeze coming off the Channel.

'"It's all wrong!" she shouted above the wind. "Won't somebody do something?"

'I dashed across the scrub, stumbling into a dratted bunker, determined to help. However, when I approached and she turned to face me, I realised it was none other than Miss Hardwicke! I grabbed her in my arms. I must say she was in a state of some disarray, her arms flailing about wildly, her lack of decent feminine attire most unbecoming in a young lady. I cried, "Miss Hardwicke, what are you doing up here? What on earth has happened to you?"

'She struggled and broke free but before she disappeared into the mist she screamed, "Cuckmere Haven, the coastguard cottages, please hurry!" By now the mist was fast enveloping the headland and the golf links besides.'

'One moment, Brocklehurst.' Holmes took out his pocket book and a lead pencil, passing it across to the patient. 'I require a sketch of the area of the golf links and the point upon the cliffs you encountered Miss Hardwicke. Mark out the link where the coastal footpath runs, will you?'

'Very well,' said he, taking but a short time to compose a rough map and returning the items forthwith before continuing his narrative.

'She screamed, I heard her in the distance, but I decided to make my way forthwith to the coastguard cottage. I have known this landmark since a child and had no difficulty locating the place. I was greeted at the door by a woman dressed from head to toe in black.

'"Are you Edward?" she asked, with a curious expression, full of sympathy. She led me inside the dwelling where I saw the coastguard was sat before the hearth reading his paper, a fine view of the Channel visible from the sitting-room window.

'"Edward? No, I am Peregrine Brocklehurst," said I, somewhat put out by her doting manner.

'"This way if you please, sir." We passed along a corridor to a darkened room at the end. Mourning crêpe shrouded every mirrored surface and a memoriam candle upon the black draped mantelpiece cast flickering shadows. I was at once confronted by an open, lidless coffin containing the corpse of Miss Hardwicke, who resembled a perfect waxwork.'

'I think I have enough to be getting along with, thank you, Mr Brocklehurst,' said my companion, stretching out his long legs beneath the table and relighting his pipe. 'We all of us of course fully sympathise with your terrible experience. But let us

116

not dwell further upon the more sombre aspects of your predicament. I propose that myself and Doctor Watson shall take the next available train and venture to Seaford. We shall report back here at the Garland at nine sharp tomorrow morning. Meanwhile, Felix, you shall prepare the release papers, for this young man need not be detained in your wing for much longer.'

'This is outrageous,' laughed Doctor Proust, 'I only meant that you should be shown a classic case of a psychotic delusionist, one who is prone to audible and visual hallucinations, a form of mania.'

'My dear Felix, who are we to judge as to where and whom cupid's arrow chooses to strike? If it is a Pullman carriage on the London to Brighton – so be it!'

'This is patently absurd, Mr Holmes. The man is a complete obsessive. "Miss Hardwicke", if she even exists, probably cares nothing for his feelings. Peregrine is fooling himself, he imagines love and marriage to hinge entirely on a one and a half hour train journcy.'

'Felix, we have known each other for a while now. Trust me upon this matter. If I am wrong I shall be first to admit that as a consulting detective I have overstepped the mark. But from what I have heard so far, I believe poor Brocklehurst to have been the victim of a number of coincidences overlapping one another. There is a way forward but I shall need time to investigate. My conclusions will ultimately, I hope, lead to a happy outcome.'

* * *

Thus began our Sussex adventure. From London we changed trains at Lewes and continued along the branch to Seaford, alighting at the seaside terminus in good spirits and with a spring in our step, for the weather was glorious with not a cloud in prospect. Together we walked through the town to the esplanade and thence made our way to the golf club at Seaford Head, the mountainous links clearly visible from afar, a group of members teeing off at the clubhouse.

'Young Peregrine is in a delicate state of health,' said I, pausing to take stock. 'I should be inclined to give him a month's confinement at least. Your prognosis is maybe a trifle optimistic.'

'By Jove, Watson, you medical fellows are certainly as thick as thieves. Bye the bye, how do you know he and Miss Hardwicke are not in love? That all he infers is in fact correct, a chance meeting leads to a blossoming relationship – marriage and a happy home?'

'You of all people – what piffling nonsense!' I chuckled. 'But you are perfectly correct, Holmes, I should not judge this poor fellow's character too harshly. The Brocks are certainly well known hereabouts in Sussex and the elder brother stands to inherit the title "Lord of the Manor", the house at Westdene, the lands and estate, worth millions. As is customary, the younger son Peregrine shall get nothing. This is how the great landed gentry of England works.'

By now we had reached the breezy brow of the cliff and headed directly across the links to the bunker to which Brocklehurst had earlier referred.

Holmes retrieved his pocket book and studied the roughly sketched map carefully.

'We have already, at Doctor Proust's interview I trust, established that there were identical twin sisters involved.'

'Twins? It had crossed my mind, certainly,' said I.

'One sister apparently fell to her death from the headland, plunging two hundred feet or so, while the other all of a sudden returns from France, perhaps entirely unaware of the tragedy. What we must find out, my dear Watson, is the precise nature of the woman's death, given that all indications point to foul play, for did not Miss Hardwicke call out from this spot the entreaty, "It's all wrong, won't somebody do something", prior to her embrace with young Peregrine?'

'Indeed, for she must surely have had her suspicions and come over here to see for herself the awful place her identical twin fell to her death.'

'And may have actually had some inkling of the method, but no real proof, hence her evident frustration. Hallo, I recall mention of the sea mists, the coastal fogs that encroach upon the headland so frequently at this time of year, no doubt shrouding the golf course and causing play to be abandoned.'

'Poor visibility would make this an unsafe place to walk, given the close proximity of the cliff edge,' said I. 'There is evidently no post and wire fence, a row of chalk stones suffice to show the way.'

'By Jove Watson, that's it! See the tussocky grass over here where I am lining up my cane, counting the yardage?'

My friend knelt perilously close to the cliff edge, peering down at the sheer chalk face where rocky ledges provided nesting sites for squawking gulls and their young. 'What if somebody came up here when it was foggy and shifted the stones used to mark off the coastal path, thus causing a determined walker usually guided by such white stones in poor visibility to stumble over the edge, plunging to certain death on the rocky outcrop below?'

'It is a strong possibility,' said I, fully conceding this was most likely the case. While I stepped forward to join my companion viewing the pounding surf from that great height, a number of gulls took flight, swooping inland above the clubhouse.

Holmes suddenly became animated, for like me he had noticed something glinting below; the remnants of a broken bottle caught on a ledge, the strong sunlight at that moment reflecting on, and picking out, various twinkling shards of green glass.

'I must obtain what remains of that bottle,' he mused. 'A boat shall be required to reach the overhang. Still, I should imagine there must be plenty of stout oarsmen hereabouts prepared to supply a vessel and the necessary manpower, for a sovereign or two. The sea is relatively calm after all.'

He got up and leaned on his silver-topped cane, savouring the bracing sea air.

'Whoever perpetrated this abominable murder lived close by, and was aware of the vicissitudes of the local weather. My dear Watson, at each turn this overlapping set of circumstances becomes more and more evil and connived. What manner of beast should come up here and be prepared to take another's life, a young woman in her prime, a coastguard's daughter whose twin sister Peregrine Brocklehurst has fallen in love with?'

By way of continuing our investigations, we proceeded to follow the coastal path eastwards, trudging beside open ground and large patches of elder, hawthorn and blackthorn scrub to an area known locally as Cuckmere Haven, where could be found a neat cluster of coastguard cottages perched upon the cliff, facing out to the grey-green sea, the undulating vista of the Seven Sisters close by.

Folk were at home and the coastguard, a Mr Harold Hardwicke, proved both amiable and charming company, his wife providing us with a welcome glass of stout to slake our thirst. Smoking our pipes, Holmes swiftly drew the general conversation round to the recent tragic death and funeral of his daughter the week previous. We quickly established that Emily, the twin who resided at home with the coastguard and his wife, during the last months of her life enjoyed regular walks to Seaford. She would start off at lunchtime, not returning until late evening. She passed the golf links, he confided, and yes, the fog was 'terrible thick upon the day of her death, every foghorn along the Sussex coast blowing the alert', but he emphasised his beloved daughter was well used to such weather, having been brought up as a child in this blowy coastal region.

'Do you know of an Edward Brocklehurst?' Holmes said in passing, knocking his pipe out on the brass fireguard.

'You refer to the next Lord of the Manor, I take

it,' said he, puffing on his Meerschaum, his sea boots propped up on a small stool. 'The oldest son who shall inherit a million and more in land and assets, become Master of the Foxhounds and reside at Fenhurst Place, the manor at Westdene. I do not know him personally but I did know his father Archibald Segram, and a wiser, more charitable man never lived. The house was made so beautiful and homely by generations of Brocks.'

'But what of Edward?' intervened Holmes.

'It is no secret in these parts that the older son has for some time been propositioning my daughter, having only a fortnight past sent her an expensively wrapped gift and a perfumed letter proclaiming his love interest. The Belgian chocolates, I must emphasise, were promptly returned unopened for in truth she found his persistent attentions irksome. For instance, waylaying her along the esplanade with a bouquet of roses, obviously the worse for drink. He was becoming a nuisance. Although her dear mother could not understand how Emily could throw away an opportunity to better herself and perhaps become the next Lady Brocklehurst. But my girl was adamant that she had eyes only for her new beau, a young wheelwright from Seaford who made a good, steady income and one day she hoped to marry.'

'Dear me,' Holmes said sadly. 'Jealousy – one class of person, "the gentry", of his inferior, "the commoner", so it all comes down to this. I have to tell you Mr Hardwicke, and it pains me greatly to do so, that it is my firm belief as a consulting detective that your daughter did not simply fall to her death accidentally upon the cliff that foggy day, as was reported by the papers, but was deliberately murdered.'

'Murdered! My other daughter Delia is of the same mind. You know, sir, she came back from France on Saturday last and did not learn of her twin sister's death until the wake was held. She stayed here at the cottage, she was naturally most distressed, and when I mentioned Edward's unrequited affections, she insisted the man had a reputation as a drunkard and a rake who made the lives of the servants over at Westdene intolerable, and was violent and horsewhipped old Mr Searle who looks after the kennels of the local hunt, leaving him permanently scarred, and no compensation whatsoever. But the gentry are well known for these spiteful traits, sir. Nonetheless I have always learnt to respect my betters up at the big house. Cold-blooded murder, no, I do not believe one of the sons of Archie Segram capable of such a heinous act.'

'One further point. Young Peregrine claims he saw your daughter Delia running along the footpath beside the golf links in her nightshirt. Could you elaborate?'

'Yes sir, from what I gather she was on her way to Seaford to summon a detective and voice her concerns to police. Fortunately, dear Mrs Jolliffe, who serves at the corner shop, noticed her wandering up Church Street like a demented wraith, took her in, fed her a bowl of beef broth and settled her straight to bed, for she was in no fit state to make accusations.'

'To formulate a case against Edward Brocklehurst would require evidence, not merely heartfelt conjecture. But, I tell you, Hardwicke, after listening to all you say I am inclined to take your daughter's part in this affair. I fully intend to pursue this fellow to the courts. Come Watson, we shall venture to Lewes assizes and seek out a Commissioner at the highest level. But first, I wonder if we might hire a boat from you, Mr Hardwicke, and some stout fellows to man the oars.'

How odd that what, to me at least, seemed like a pleasant interlude, eddies of water lapping against the boat, the cheerful banter of the crew as we navigated our way round the bay towards Seaford Head, the dipping oars, the steering of the tiller in calm waters, Holmes seated at the prow languidly smoking his pipe, should in fact be so crucial in obtaining a conviction, for of the fragments of glass we retrieved that day from the cliff, one curved piece bore a handsome crested label indicating the bottle had once contained a rare French Burgundy, exclusive to Crabtree's, the Soho wine merchant, which regularly supplied Fenhurst Place with cases of the noblest and finest vintages. Other shards were smothered in clear and wonderfully defined, chalky fingerprints.

What became Edward Brocklehurst's final undoing, apart from my companion's own damning contribution, was his being kept confined in a cell at Lewes Prison and deprived of his normally considerable intake of claret, Burgundy, porter and Highland whisky, which had the effect of causing him to shake uncontrollably with *delirium tremens* and at night suffer terrible visions. This, combined with intensive and relentless questioning by a detective, caused him to eventually break down and confess to the murder of Emily Hardwicke. He was later executed.

But there was an altogether brighter outcome to consider, for after a brief courtship, Delia Hardwicke and Peregrine Brocklehurst were married and together moved into Fenhurst Place at Westdene, to the great joy and delight of servants and estate workers alike, for he was now the new Squire and sole heir to his late father's considerable fortune.

9

The Deceiving Portrait

'Pray, what do you deduce from that, dear boy?' asked Sherlock Holmes, lounging on the sofa in his dressing gown smoking a cigarette, one brazenly cold morning at the beginning of January.

He tossed across a scrap of paper, thereafter resuming his ardent study of a reference work. The room was unbearably chilly because he had allowed the fire to go out. I was braced upon the bearskin rug on my hands and knees, holding a scorched sheet of newspaper over the wire fireguard in an attempt to create sufficient draught to fan the flames.

'It's cold in here,' I complained, still somewhat annoyed. 'It's winter, Holmes, our basic homely comforts depend upon the front sitting-room being kept properly warm.'

All at once the coals set alight and flames were leaping about in the grate. I basked in the welcome warmth from the fire, before perusing the scribblings of pencil on paper.

'Well, if my "prescriptions" Latin is up to scratch we have firstly: "*Ipse frangers dem sacer signum cavereum vetus doctrina et Europe magica propter hoc exsecratio famila genitor ab limbus homo lupus et suus mess creatre non deus imago vero de malus et completus luna illi: venari et vasa colligers.*" Translated, this reads, oddly: "He who breaks this sacred seal beware of the old European magic for this accursed family sired from the loins of a werewolf were created not in God's image but that of the devil and upon the full moon hunt as a pack." I cannot make head nor tail of it Holmes. Is it another of your riddles?'

'It is originally the work of a seventeenth-century stonemason Watson, the Latin inscription being carved in solid granite above a crypt entrance.'

'I'm all ears,' said I, reaching for a cigarette before striking a Vesta.

'Alas, the accompanying letter is a trifle un-enlightening. However, we do have a summons for high tea, a request from a Lady Helena Dodswell that we take a train to Wickham and visit her country seat. I've looked her up in the *Peerage* and apparently she's old-world nobility. The family goes back to Edward the Confessor. Attached is a rather generous cheque from Coutts because she writes to say she requires my services as a consulting detective. Good old Watson, are you game?'

'I should quite fancy a trip out to Wickham,' said I.

'Now, where's that Bradshaw's?' wondered Holmes, fumbling about on the shelf.

Lady Dodswell owned a charming country house on the outskirts of Gerrards Cross. South Wrexham Manor dated from the sixteenth century. L-shaped, it possessed a splendid example of a barrel-vaulted room with oriel windows and fine cusped arches. I recall we were greeted at the gatehouse by a faithful old retainer, and shown with great courtesy into the Great Hall, and thence along a panelled corridor to the drawing-room, where before a roaring log fire her Ladyship awaited our arrival keenly, with a wonderful spread laid before us for high tea. Upon entering the drawing-room both Holmes and myself were aware of a most striking portrait in oils by Holbein hung above the mighty fireplace. I could not resist the lure of stepping round the oak refectory table and taking a peek at the inscription on the ornately carved, gilded frame. 'Sir Thomas Dodswell, Duke of Stafford, awaiting execution upon Tower Hill, 1643.'

Bewigged, possessing a pallid, cruel, pox-ridden face with an obstinate jaw and more than a hint of a derisible sneer upon his bloodless lips, the Duke was about to address the mob from the scaffold. The axeman was in attendance, as were a number of nervous clergy, looking on. The sky was painted overcast, and a flock of crows circled above. The whole picture seemed to me infused with underlying menace, Holbein's use of light and shade being remarkable.

'Sir Thomas was a notorious rake, Doctor Watson, who meddled in politics and may have murdered his first wife. Oh, and before you ask, the "family" referred to in the Latin inscription I posted to your lodgings at Baker Street refers to us, the Dodswells, the Duke and his descendants are housed in the family crypt over at the chapel. Miss Foley, pour tea for the gentlemen. Mr Holmes and Doctor Watson must be famished after their train journey to Wickham.'

'Before we demolish this most delicious repast your Ladyship, I wonder if I might take a minute or two of your time to discuss the actual reason for inviting us to South Wrexham Manor. Your letter was of course discreet and I appreciate this, but if I am to act on your behalf as a consulting detective I shall require an explanation concerning the Latin inscription *Ipse frangers dem sacer.*'

Lady Dodswell dabbed her chin with a napkin. She was a robust little creature with fine silvery hair and twinkling violet blue eyes that missed nothing.

'The facts are these, Mr Holmes. The chapel housing the Duke's descendants is in a poor state of repair and for the first time in a hundred years I have allowed building and restoration work to commence. An inner door to the crypt had to be broken into. They knocked it down.'

'Hence "He who breaks the sacred seal". Pray continue.'

'Upon a moonlit night last week Miss Foley and myself were sat by the fire quietly reading our novels, whereupon a stranger appeared at the window and looked in, his edacious face flattened against the frosted glass pane.'

'Sir,' implored Miss Foley, wringing her hands together in an agitated way. 'It was not an ordinary person we saw that night, but a changeling. I have it on good authority from Mr Rochester, the head butler, who possesses an old book in which there is an indecent engraving of a similar creature. What we saw, and I can vouch a bright full moon was in progress, was a face covered in fur, not a bushy beard such as Mr Rochester wears, but a pelt more akin to an animal. It was a wolfman.'

'"Upon the full moon hunt as a pack." A pack, madam. You cannot deny Miss Foley that your argument is flawed for it was not a group of persons, or changelings, if you prefer, gathered at the window, but a solitary intruder.'

'I might be able to offer a plausible explanation,' said I, filling my plate with delicately cut cucumber sandwiches.

'A wolfman, werewolf, changeling, what difference does it make? Merely a Germanic fairy-tale creature,' sighed Holmes, taking a cup to his lips and sipping the hot tea. 'Children's authors will concoct such ludicrous fantasies, but in the real world it's nonsense.'

'They exist. What about the Latin inscription? How do you explain its warning, Mr Holmes?' asked Miss Foley.

'Now, now, my dear, let the genial Doctor Watson get a word in edgeways.' Lady Dodswell chided her favourite servant, giving her an indulgent smile.

'Miss Foley has a point,' I said. 'The extensive facial hair is in fact in medical terminology referred to as "lupine lycanthropy". I have myself never encountered a patient suffering from this rare condition, but my medical dictionary devotes a whole page to the subject.'

Holmes sighed. 'My dear fellow, medical references aside, what we have here is clearly an effective means of disguise, a clever means of concealing the true identity of whoever was peering so intently into the drawing-room that evening.'

'Mr Holmes, such a practical and sensible explanation,' said her Ladyship. 'Your calm, logical thinking is most welcome in this turgid affair. I too share this view. I am loath to embrace the fantastical and prefer to believe our "window watcher" was an ordinary person who for whatever reason wished to conceal their identity. Now gentlemen, let's leave this sordid subject for a while and enjoy our meal.'

For the remainder of tea we talked of much more homely topics but Lady Dodswell did let slip a family secret which caused considerable amusement.

'At ninety-three,' she confessed, 'I have outlived my husband, my daughter and my eldest son. Their remains are kept here, secure.'

'You of course refer to the small chapel on the estate we saw earlier,' said I. 'A most charming location if I may say so. The crypt where Thomas the Duke of Stafford is buried.'

'No, I refer to the sideboard, Doctor Watson,' she replied sternly. 'For each of the cremation urns are clearly labelled and when I depart this uncertain world we shall all of us be united in the rose garden. The chapel crypt is already full enough of old ancestral bones and I'd hate to share space with you-know-who.'

'Forgive me,' said Holmes, 'your youngest son St Stevas was killed in a mountaineering accident climbing the Eiger was he not? He was last seen at the summit at about three o'clock in the afternoon in poor weather and bad visibility. The mountain rescue team were alerted but the search was later called off. He was accompanied by Lord Lumley and Harold Finsbury-West. I recall reading in *The*

Times about the tragedy which occurred only a year or two ago, did it not?'

'St Stevas was always my husband's favourite, Mr Holmes.' Her Ladyship was doing her best to conceal her raw emotions. 'Although strangely enough of a totally different temperament, opposites if you will, St Stevas, open and gregarious, my husband dour, buttoned up and stiff upper-lipped, yet the two, despite this, got on rather well, and after his death on the Eiger, my husband's health quickly deteriorated and he was himself dead but a month after we received that awful letter from the Swiss Embassy, a double blow being the fact they were never able to locate the body. You may recall Lord Lumley was beside himself with genuine grief and guilt for he blamed himself at the time for not looping a knot in the climbing rope properly. Harold Finsbury-West, or "Fins" as he was known, said it was all nonsense and down to poor visibility and bad luck. Anyhow St Stevas died doing what he loved best – mountaineering.'

It was at this juncture, during a lull in conversation while we filled our pipes, that I chose to comment upon the aforementioned Holbein portrait of the Duke of Stafford above the fireplace.

'The Duke's brown eyes are mesmerising,' said I, lighting my pipe. 'They follow you around the room. Even now at high tea I can almost sense him gazing at me from the scaffold as we speak. The painting must seem quite intimidating by candlelight your Ladyship.'

'Brown, Doctor Watson?'

'Pardon me?'

'Brown eyes? Surely you are mistaken. The eyes of the Duke are a rheumy blue in colour. I have known that particular painting since childhood.' She turned very pale, gripping the ebony handle of her cane so tightly it bleached her knuckles white. 'Mr Holmes,' she stuttered, 'could you please verify?'

'A second opinion? Of course, Lady Dodswell.' My esteemed colleague leapt up from his chair and went straight over to the fireplace. He spent some time examining the portrait with his magnifying lens.

'Unfortunately I fear upon this occasion I must fully concur with Doctor Watson. The Duke's eyes are brown – penetratingly so.'

'Then it must be a forgery.'

'Before rushing to conclusions, might I ask if there are any further distinguishing marks? On the back panel for instance?'

'A crack, a fissure running along the length of the frame,' she said decisively.

Stood precariously balanced upon a chair, checking the back panel, my companion shook his head grimly.

'No marks, not one crack. The wood looks fairly new, partly smoothed with a rough grade of sandpaper. The panel appears flawless.'

'Confirmation!' gasped her ladyship, reaching for a glass of water Miss Foley had poured from a jug. 'Oh, my failing sight! My eyes are not what they once were. Fetch my opera glasses Foley. The original Holbein has been stolen from my house, Mr Holmes. If not for Doctor Watson's off-chance remark I should have been none the wiser. I should have remained ignorant. The pigment, varnish and details, apart from the use of the wrong colour paint for the eyes, are outstanding.'

'Absolutely! The brushwork matches the Old Master's exactly. Only an expert should be able to judge it a fraud, I'm certain of it. A most talented criminal is at work here. His commission fee would have been substantial.'

'An art forger of outstanding ability,' said I.

'I'm going to make a bold assertion,' said Holmes, standing back with his hands held behind him. 'I'm going to plump for the Swiss forger Jakob Tinguely, the greatest living imitator of the Old Masters, alone capable of such a breathtaking deception.'

'But how on earth did this art thief manage to break into my house?' exclaimed her Ladyship. 'To swap the pictures, I mean.'

Foley grasped the handles of her mistress's wheeled invalid carriage and propelled it closer to the fire. Lady Dodswell placed a shawl across her shoulders, cradled her face in her hands, and started to weep.

Holmes knelt down and gently took her gnarled old hand in his, anxious to placate her.

'Your Ladyship, on the night of the full moon when you told us this stranger whose face was covered in hair or fur peered in at the window, the disguised fellow was real flesh and blood – not a changeling affected by the lunar cycle as Mr Rochester would have us believe. He stared in at the window and unsettled you. What if he was in fact assessing the position of the Holbein portrait hung above the fireplace?'

'Indeed?'

135

'What if it was familiar to him?'

'Familiar? I'm sorry, I don't quite follow.'

'St Stevas may be alive, Lady Dodswell, for would he not possess, even after all this time, a key to one of the doors of South Wrexham Manor?'

'Preposterous! The very notion is disagreeable and hurtful to the extreme, sir! I must ask both you and Doctor Watson to leave my house this instant. I shall ring for the servants to escort you off my property. You have struck at my heart Mr Holmes, as sure as any bullet from a revolver.'

My companion withdrew and bowed slightly.

'I will not rest until I have found your son, your Ladyship. You may set your dogs on myself and Doctor Watson, but it changes nothing. The Swiss connection is too strong. The Swiss forger Jakob Tinguely – how was he contacted, how was he paid? What value can be placed on a portrait by Holbein? A considerable sum I'll wager. A collector would pay almost any amount of money to possess such a masterpiece.'

'The audacity! Get out, the pair of you!' she screamed. 'How dare you intimate my son is still alive and, worse, capable of money grubbing and thievery? To talk ill of the dead in such a cold-hearted way – you are a heartless scoundrel, Mr Holmes.'

'On the contrary. I see only the straightforward facts before me. We shall trouble you no further, your Ladyship. I apologise profusely for upsetting you so, but I shall see this matter through to the bitter end. Good evening.'

* * *

Returning to Baker Street that night, it was bitterly cold but Mrs Hudson had made sure our rooms were warm and comfortable and I was glad to be once more ensconced at my desk, for with limpid gas globes turned fully up we were a hive of activity, all available space taken over by numerous press cuttings, maps of Europe, copiously written notes, filing indices in disarray, travel books on Switzerland, and our Continental gazetteer. In short, we were each of us consumed by Holmes's obsessive quest to locate by any means Lady Helena Dodswell's son St Stevas, and correspondingly gather any information we could on Lord Lumley and Harold Finsbury-West, for in my companion's mind at least they had deliberately assisted him in the faking of his own death.

'Holmes,' said I, 'what on earth put you on to this in the first place? The old dame is livid and you've burnt all your bridges so far as the Dodswells are concerned, that's for sure.'

'My dear fellow, do you recall mention of the "Lombard Street Crash" a few years back? In one sweep a syndicate of investment brokers in the City with vast fortunes of other people's money gambled on the Stock Exchange and lost the lot – left with nothing but accumulated debts?'

'"The Lombard Street *Massacre*". Wasn't that what the papers called it at the time?'

'By Jove, yes, and weren't those investors hit hard? St Stevas was one of the brokers involved. His personal fortune was decimated.'

'And you knew this all along?'

'Indeed, I knew about the financial shenanigans,

certainly. Pass me the Persian slipper dear boy, and pour us both a whiskey and seltzer, we're going to have a late night of it I'm afraid, and we must be up bright and early.'

'Oh? Why's that?' said I, filling our glasses.

'We are to travel to Switzerland. Why, I should quite fancy a spell in Europe. Don't look so downhearted, many of us British travel there at this time of year to take advantage of the winter sports.'

'There's something behind all of this, Holmes. Pray, what aren't you telling me?' I ejaculated.

'Ha! Elementary, my dear Watson. By consulting all available data concerning the three friendly mountaineers, it emerges that all were habitually drawn to the Junger region of Switzerland at this time of year, to the slopes of Grindelwald, in particular.'

'Oh? Why was that?'

'To ski.'

'That's quite a new fad, isn't it?'

'Not for the Norwegians, Watson. From a very young age they are adept at skis and used to covering great distances in the snow. With the single pole, they manage to glide along most effectively. For us British I grant you it is a relatively new leisure activity, but it is quickly catching on. I believe Lord Lumley learnt to ski competently in Norway and passed on his skills to the other two.'

We arrived off the train at Grindelwald, nestling within the craggy trio of the Wetterhorn, Mettenberg and Eiger mountains, in the early hours of Tuesday morning, settled in and made our base the Gletschergarten Hotel. After a first-rate breakfast, we headed for the resort lodge. I confess I felt quite excited to be in Switzerland again. The valley air was sparkling and crisp, while tightly packed snow crunched beneath our heels as we trudged east along the village main street, lined with attractive Alpine chalet-style shops, selling all manner of goods.

The *tabac* proved irresistible, and both of us surveyed the fine array of Swiss pipes in the window – long, curved stems, carved bowls with tassels and hinged caps – but Holmes had his eye on one pipe in particular.

We bustled in off the snowy street, the doorbell clanging merrily.

'The village of Grindelwald is charming,' said I. 'But what of St Stevas, Holmes?'

While in the shop my friend seemed relaxed, to be almost indifferent. He appeared to me to hardly care, yet from our many previous adventures I knew this nonchalant attitude was misleading, for in truth his magnificent brain was always alert and thinking through possibilities.

'Watson, tomorrow we shall seek out the English community who live in the village the whole year round. St Stevas should not be difficult to trace. Ah, may I have a half pound of your excellent tobacco from *that* jar, and I spied a most inviting calabash pipe in the window. Might I purchase that also?'

The *tabac* shop owner, a jolly fellow, smiled warmly as he took down the jar, adjusting the scales.

'Of course, my dear sir. You are both of you Englanders?'

'Indeed, from London,' said I, choosing a selection of cigars from the display cabinet beneath the counter.

'More and more of you come to the resort. The ladies in groups, the men also. In the last few years the sport of skiing has become "all the rage", as you Britishers say. My son Heinrich is an instructor, yes, and in the summer months he's a walking guide above the village around Männlichen and Pfingstegg.'

'An instructor?'

'Just so.' The shop owner wrapped up our purchases and took our money, placing it in the till with a flourish.

'I am fairly adept with skis, but my friend here is a total incompetent. Might I trouble you for a card?' asked Holmes.

'Certainly. Heinrich starts on the beginners' slopes at half past nine. You can practise all day. Just take the path to the resort lodge where the tourists gather for the cable car. You will find him there.'

'We are most indebted to you for your time. Good day,' said I, doffing my cap.

'Enjoy your calabash pipe, sir. A fine smoke. I myself possess one.'

'Thank you. I shall be taking this one back to London with me.'

The afternoon was spent practising and, thanks to the kindly patience and perseverance of Herr Heinrich, I had at least mastered the basic co-ordination between Norwegian skis and the single pole required to take to the slopes, albeit hesitantly and with many a tumble. However, I was to enjoy something of a baptism of fire for, while taking a breather, enjoying a hot chocolate on a bench in front of the resort lodge, I observed my companion was peering intently through his binoculars.

'Holmes!' I called out, 'is it a cable car you're looking at?'

'Watson,' said he excitedly, beckoning me over. 'Tell me what you can determine when you focus on Grindelwald Grund railway station. See the tiny, bright red two-coach train? Now, move along to the left, a fellow approaching the ticket hall.'

'Good heavens, Holmes,' I cried. 'The person's carrying a brown paper parcel under his arm that corresponds in size to the missing Holbein!'

'Precisely, dear boy. However, we have no way of telling whether it's St Stevas, because he's wearing a substantial ski parka with a fur hood, popular with the local Swiss.'

'The train's pulling out Holmes. We've lost him. Come, have a chocolate drink and relax. We can't compete with a mountain railway.'

'On the contrary, my dear Watson. Strap on your skis.'

'My dear fellow, I am only a beginner!'

'If we take to the slopes now we have a fair chance of catching up with the Kleine–Sheidegg train at the next stop, where we can with luck intercept our suspect passenger and get a closer look at him.'

I hurriedly strapped on my broad mountain skis and joined Holmes, who was prepared and ready, a woollen cap pulled well down over his head. This was not the time to question my own modest abilities, or feel apprehensive.

'Watson, old fellow, see that group of young ladies

further down the slope, dressed in the long ski skirts of a thick, tough fabric? That's the route we're taking. Don't prod that pole of yours into the snow so jerkily, allow yourself to fly along.'

With a swish of skis we were off. I can report, although I fell hard on my backside often, bruising my rump, and my legs felt stiff and sore for weeks afterwards, we did indeed beat the train to the next stop. And I was heartily congratulated by my erstwhile colleague, which pleased me greatly.

The red two-coach train arrived a good five minutes after we were ourselves waiting on the platform. Our luck was in, for the gentleman in question, wearing the fur parka, alighted and walked towards us, his face for the most part concealed by a thick hood.

'Good evening,' said my companion, seizing the fellow's arm. 'You know, I'm determined to get a local artist to paint my nephew. Could you recommend anyone? I couldn't help noticing you have a framed picture under your arm. Am I being nosey?'

'Not at all,' said a pleasant voice from inside the fur hood. 'You're English, aren't you? In fact I've just had this portrait of my wife framed at the shop in Grindelwald and collected it earlier. There's a good local artist, Franz Vogel. Here, let's go into the waiting room and I'll write down the address. Has either of you a pencil?'

'May I?' asked Holmes, taking the parcel and placing it carefully on a bench.

'Slide the brown paper off by all means. Have a look,' said he in a relaxed way, taking out a card and scribbling on the back. 'That's a Vogel. It's a good likeness – Hetta, my little blonde wife, will be delighted.'

Holmes appeared somewhat crestfallen. He couldn't hide his initial disappointment, for the stolen portrait of Thomas Dodswell, the Duke of Stafford, this wasn't. Neither could he accuse our genial, waylaid English passenger of anything remotely criminal, at least until he entirely innocently removed his fur hood. Then we were both left in a state of profound shock.

'Good gracious,' said Holmes, 'you're St Stevas. I recall your photograph in *The Times*. A little chubbier about the face perhaps, a receding hairline, but it's you!'

'I don't deny it.'

'Explain your disappearance two years ago, man. We're not policemen or Interpol, anything you say will be treated in the strictest confidence.'

'Very well. I gambled badly on the Stock Exchange and lost a fortune because of it. I had no other option. There were creditors at every turn.'

'Was Lord Lumley in on this?'

'Certainly. It was he who initially suggested I might disappear in the Bernese Alps. Harold Finsbury-West agreed it was for the best. We were, after all, each of us skilled mountaineers and had a pretty good idea of the final route I should take.'

'Your companions alerted the mountain rescue team that you were missing and told them you had fallen to your death on the Eiger. They were thus fellow conspirators.'

'Exactly.'

'I instinctively knew it was you staring in at the window that night, presumably hatching a plan to swap the valuable painting for a fake. South Wrexham Manor was after all your family home. Did it hurt your conscience?'

'It was a hard decision certainly, but I needed the money. The Holbein represented my only way back to my old life. I mean, I should never have returned to England, but here in Switzerland I have a new identity and a lovely little wife to look after. I had a key and let myself in through the pantry door.'

'The forgery is a Jakob Tinguely.'

'The best money can buy.'

'That must have been an expensive commitment.'

'Lord Lumley paid for it, and I can assure you he has done very nicely out of it – a sound investment. We are all still the dearest of friends and have known each other since Eton. That shows you how far back we go. "Fins" was the best man at my wedding.'

'Do you have any regard for the emotional cost?' said I, incensed, fed up with this filthy polite charade. 'Your poor father never recovered from your loss. Lady Dodswell, that most kind and noble of gentry, what must she have gone through? You are a bounder sir, a cad.'

'But alive.'

'What do you mean?'

'I should explain. My losses were not only incurred on the Stock Exchange. I had amassed gambling debts at my club to the tune of £50,000. I had to run for my life. Now, looking back, it seems pitiable, pathetic and, yes, I do regret the loss of my father, for we were very close. But, which would you prefer, that over breakfast he read about my body having been dredged out of the Thames, mutilated and in a canvas sack, having to identify the remains at Wapping?'

'I should tell you, St Stevas,' said my companion, opening his cigarette case and passing them round, 'my name is Sherlock Holmes. I am a consulting detective and this is my colleague Doctor Watson. It's my part in this affair to represent your mother, Lady Dodswell. Is it too late for me to retrieve the Holbein? Tell me that.'

St Stevas smoked his cigarette for a while before answering. 'I'm afraid so, Mr Holmes. I've banked the money. Once again I'm a fairly wealthy man.'

'Your client's satisfied.'

'Completely so. He returned to Zurich last night.'

'Why don't you allow me to explain to your mother, in complete confidence, the reasons why you had to flee the country, fake your own death? The portrait of the Duke of Stafford on Tower Hill is valuable. But your relationship with your mother must surely rank higher. Have you any children?'

'Two girls, Grunhilda and Lette.'

'Come man, discretion can be assured. You have my word, and that of my colleague Doctor Watson. It is my bounden duty to report back to Lady Dodswell to tell her that you are alive and well. I promised her that.'

'My dear sir.' He grasped Holmes's hand warmly. 'It has now been two years since my exile. Nothing would please me or my darling little wife more than being reunited with Ma. If my mother and myself could somehow be reconciled I should be eternally grateful.'

'My dear Mr Holmes, I am honestly glad the portrait is gone. The Duke of Stafford shall no longer look down on us so scathingly from the scaffold on Tower Hill. The room feels lighter without that wicked old devil dominating the wall space. I cannot thank you both enough. Miss Foley and myself leave for Switzerland tomorrow morning, to travel, explore, but primarily to stop off and visit my grandchildren. St Stevas, I mean Herr Muller of Grindelwald and his wife, Hetta, await our arrival. My heart is so full I can barely speak.'

I took a sip of tea and glanced at my colleague, lounging upon the couch and smoking his newly acquired calabash pipe with evident relish, wreaths of smoke curling up to the ceiling and forming a hazy fug around the chandelier.

'The Constable landscape suits the drawing-room admirably, your Ladyship,' said he at length. 'The grazing sheep, the old water mill, the hayrick and the flowing stream enhance the rustic scene wonderfully.'

'Oh, I agree, Mr Holmes. I brought the painting in from the hallway, and I think it suits the fireplace rather well.'

9

The Balcombe Horror

After shaving and dressing one morning in late
April, I heard a gentle tap at my bedroom door
and Mrs Hudson entered and placed a large brown
paper package, erroneously addressed to a 'Mr
Procter Dotson' in wax crayon, upon the rumpled
eiderdown.

'Oh my, it's a warm day Doctor, what a joy to see
the sunshine. I've a nice steak and kidney pudding
planned for lunch and there's the fruit tart to finish,
but you must be out of your rooms, the both of
you, by ten so I can start my cleaning.'

I hastily put the covers to rights, plumped my
pillow and straightened my bottle of Taylors lime
aftershave, shaving brush and bar of soap above the
enamel sink before adjourning to our sun-drenched,
commodious sitting-room, with its well-permeated
aroma of seasoned tobacco, to smoke a first pipe
of the day and peruse the morning editions which
my companion, as usual, discarded and piled up
beside my armchair.

Sherlock Holmes and myself would normally, over
a second pot of strong coffee, discuss the issues of
the day making headlines, the cricket scores and of

course any unusual or interesting crimes perpetrated in the metropolis, but that morning Mrs Hudson had chosen to have her annual spring clean, thus our bachelor routine had gone to the dogs.

'That's a heavyweight package, Watson,' murmured my companion, stooped over his desk with his gum brush, examining a mass of file cuttings, desperate to make a neat job of cataloguing the varied newspaper articles and get them stowed away before we were turfed out and Mrs Hudson's onslaught of dusting and tidying began in earnest at ten.

'Indeed, Holmes.'

I balanced the package on my knees and tugged as hard as I could at the taut string.

'Why do people go to the bother of tying such damnably difficult knots?' I remarked, incensed.

'Because it prevents the package from breaking open in transit, dear boy,' came the obvious retort. My friend's eyes gleamed mischievously. 'Who's it from?'

'Holmes, I'm getting there.'

I impatiently seized a pair of scissors and cut away, until at last the brown paper was torn asunder, revealing a neat leather case embossed in gold leaf. There was a note attached.

I burst out into a hearty chuckle. 'Holmes, do you remember Lance?'

'Yes, Lance Keeble, the over-ambitious young man who was an amateur photographer. His hefty glass negative plates and those infernal wooden box cameras of his with the brass lenses! I well recall helping him shift his photographic machinery from the dog cart to the rectory's front room, altogether a most vexing and exhausting afternoon. But the vicar of Balcombe Church was a most eccentric old soul. What was his name, Watson?'

'The Reverend C.W. Warbourton. Well, actually the old chap has just died, Holmes. He had a good innings though, at four and ninety, and passed away peacefully, according to this short note from St Celia's Anglican Home for Retired Clergy at Bexhill. The matron writes that he has bequeathed us generously that odd instrument of his.'

'Say no more,' said Holmes frowning. Dressed in his black frock coat he sprang to his feet and seized his long cherry wood pipe from the rack on the mantelpiece. 'I won't hear another mention of that infernal trumpet!'

'My dear fellow,' said I, 'there's no need to be so exclusive in your embarrassment. I was as dumb-founded as the rest, and that included young Lance who, after all, came out rather the worst in the affair, for he was hoping to secure his professional reputation and find a certain amount of fame through the published *Psychic Society Journal*.'

My companion filled his pipe with stale dottles of tobacco from the Persian slipper, lighting the charred bowl with a taper, and frantically puffed away. I could see by the way he was smoking that the memory of that night at Balcombe taunted the faculties of his reasoning mind to the extreme and decided to avoid further confrontation by not mentioning that 'infernal trumpet' again.

While he proceeded to sort out his newspaper cuttings I thus discreetly removed the instrument case to my bedroom and deposited it underneath the bed beside a cracked porcelain chamber pot.

However, for the discerning reader whose interest has been whetted, after Mrs Hudson had done with her cleaning and I had an hour or two to spare at my writing desk, and Holmes was scraping away on his violin behind his closed door, I decided to write an account of the so far unchronicled events of that infamous night at Balcombe.

It all began when a bold and determined young man of, I should say, one and twenty, wearing a smart dark coat and cravat with a diamond pin, barged into our rooms. I think it was a spring evening in 1881. Like many young bucks of the day he was prone to slavishly follow the fashions of Prince Albert and wore long, bushy side whiskers and a moustache, his hair combed in a certain style.

The problem as I saw it from the first with young Lance Keeble was that he was too darned pushy, an entrepreneurial fellow who didn't know when to stop! The sort of fellow you want to box around the ears to shut them up. But in the end you have to admire their sheer unremitting resolve, their ability to browbeat you round to their way of thinking.

However, on this occasion Mr Sherlock Holmes was to get the better of him.

'As an added incentive,' Keeble began, ' I will offer you five pounds if you would be good enough to accompany me to Balcombe, where history shall be made. Everything is in place, I merely require that you, Mr Holmes, and you, Doctor Watson, act as witnesses.'

'You're a young spark, Keeble,' said Holmes, putting his pipe aside and leaning forward in his chair irritably, assessing our visitor with an unrelenting, steely gaze. 'And I must say what a nerve you've got coming up unannounced to our rooms and waving a five pound note under my nose. I can make twenty times that amount from a few hours consultancy work, and I've said it before, because I recall your wretched bunch of letters, of which I answered the first, concisely and conclusively, I am *not*, repeat *not*, interested one jot in supernatural matters. I am not a psychic detective, I am a consulting detective who deals with real-life crime in the metropolis and beyond. I explained this all in my letter, Keeble, but still you have the gall to come calling at Baker Street. It won't do.'

'Lance,' said I, readily sympathising, for I understood the sound drubbing the poor fellow was presently receiving from my esteemed colleague, whom I fear had left him speechless and on the verge of tears. 'Mr Holmes is not short of a few bob. Just stick your five pound note back in your wallet and then you can take your sweetheart to the theatre or out to dinner. Now start again, but this time don't speak so fast. Give us all the relevant facts but without the spiel. You mentioned this vicar fellow, er, what was it, that rustic instrument of his? Be good enough to elaborate. Here, have a cigarette. That's it, take your time and settle in.'

'Very well, Doctor Watson,' said he contritely. 'One close and humid evening prior to a violent thunderstorm and much needed rain, I dined at my club after attending a lively session with the attractive medium Miss Florence Kent, who claimed she could materialise the spirit child Rosamund, a ten-year-old girl capable of predicting the future.

'Miss Kent impressed many observers in Northampton but failed to advance her career any further by coming down to London with her strident mother and visiting the Psychical Research Society, whence under the strictest test conditions Sir Oliver Trent no less declared her an outright fraud. The girl used that typical old ploy – the inflatable rubber dummy, with a foot pump attachment.

'During my roast beef dinner I received a message. The Rev. C.W. Warbourton was waiting to see me. I hastened into the smoking room, only to find a country parson wearing an old-fashioned black cocked hat, Steenkirk tie of fine white linen, frock coat and gaiters, sitting over by the fireplace reading the *Church Times.*

'"A rare parochial antiquity used in olden times to keep the supernatural at bay in country churchyards. Interested Mr Keeble?"

'"You have come about my advert in *The Telegraph*," I replied, "requesting unusual else rare ceremonial artefacts connected with that same subject."

'The cleric took a sip of port. "Quite so." He savoured the fine bouquet for a moment. "The artefact was used widely by sextons in the seventeenth century to ward off evil, when of course the threat of vampires, weremen, ancient wraiths and their unholy procession of shrouds, grave goblins and other lesser churchyard phenomena such as corpse candles or will-o'-the-wisp was very real. There was I suppose an openness to such things, lamentably lacking in this modern age of gaslight, but then Mr Keeble you are a junior member of the Psychic Society. I must bore you with such trifles."

' "Not at all,' I replied, lighting a cigar and tossing the spent match aside. "You speak with some authority," I acknowledged, "but tell me, what is this fascinating artefact – perhaps a straw head like the one in Wimbourne, Hampshire? Am I on the right track?"

' "Not really." The parson was somewhat dismissive. "I read recently about the *Blocksberg Tryst,* an old manuscript purported to hold the key to transcendental magic. The Society I believe has shown great interest in this document. I regard it and the 'straw head' with equal disdain. They are both in my opinion nothing more than cheap theatrical props."

' "And yours is the genuine article?" '

' "Indeed," answered the parson with a nod.

' "Ah, then perhaps it is a vamping cross?" I said smugly.

' "Not one of those either. By the way, there is only one remaining vamping cross in the country and that resides in Gloucester. The curator refuses to put it under glass and sadly one of the leather thongs is damaged."

'He took another timid sip of port. "No, my own modest contribution consists of a musical instrument made from the lid of a leaden coffin belonging to a medieval archbishop, the mouthpiece fashioned from the thigh bone of Saint Agnes of Constantinople. It is called a 'horror horn', but it is really more of a trumpet."

' "Most fascinating. May I enquire if you have brought it along with you?"

' "Oh dear me, no." The parson took a pinch of snuff up his nose. "But you are most welcome to a practical demonstration at my church in Balcombe, Mr Keeble. You are free to test it under strict laboratory conditions. The horror horn is far from being a mere redundant antiquity kept under lock and key."

' "I should be delighted."

' "Next Thursday is April the thirtieth, the eve of Mayday, else in Germany *Walpurgisnacht*, when witches celebrate their Sabbat. Bring your witnesses and, of course, photographic cameras, for I promise you shall not be disappointed. Whatever wicked spells the witches decide to dispatch at us upon the night of *Walpurgis*, my angel's trumpet shall prevail." '

I can relate that after this discourse, whilst Lance was relaxing with a whiskey and soda, I offered Holmes one of my cigarettes and observed my companion seemed satisfied that there was some element of intrigue in the young man's story.

'Do you think he's genuine, this C.W. Warbourton?' he asked, steepling his long bony fingers beneath his chin. 'I mean, all that prattle about vamping crosses and straw heads – a trumpet that possesses some sort of power to defeat evil?'

'He is an expert,' exclaimed Lance. 'Mr Holmes, only a man of letters who has spent a lifetime studying supernatural lore could possibly possess such an all-encompassing knowledge of ancient ceremonial artefacts. I believed every word.'

'However,' Holmes wagged his finger, 'he didn't

actually show you the horror horn. You've no idea what it actually looks like. I mean, from the description it sounds like a music hall prop. My instincts tell me that this reverend gentleman could possibly have connections to the Magic Circle. That's a London club of magicians, if you will, top illusionists who, by the clever use of mirrors, sulphur lamps, electricity and lantern slides can create incredible stage effects, as myself and Doctor Watson can verify after visiting a show starring the New York magician Magneto Pons at the Wimbourne Theatre in Drury Lane last year.'

'Oh, I saw the same production,' said young Keeble, excitedly. 'The whole audience left the theatre in a palpable state of stunned silence. The visuals beggared belief.'

'Exactly, so what this clergyman fellow, apparently a country parson from Balcombe promises, from what you say Keeble, and this is only conjecture, is a confrontation between the forces of good and evil, where he gets to play this mystical trumpet of his. Is that a fair summary?'

'It's a brilliant summary, if I may say so, Mr Holmes,' said Lance, beaming. 'And you will accompany me as witnesses to Balcombe on April the thirtieth?'

'Certainly, my dear boy. I shouldn't miss it for the world.'

Upon leaving the train at Balcombe, one is quickly on the densely wooded forest ridge of Sussex. Balcombe has a simple church protected by a screen of Scotch firs. The rectory overlooks the trim and tidy churchyard. There is barely a quarter hour passes from morning till night without the rumble of a locomotive on the main line to Brighton, which passes through the midst of this wild game region before plunging into the long tunnel.

Thus it was I arrived at Balcombe railway station at three o'clock accompanied by my colleague, Mr Sherlock Holmes. Young Keeble went on ahead, the station luggage cart stacked high with photographic equipment, while we simply trudged along the lane to the clergyman's house part-way into the village.

It was a warm, sunny afternoon. Birdsong and the lazy drone of bumble bees made our short journey to the rectory all the more enjoyable.

We received lunch in the dining-room and after a delicious meal, all good rustic fare, the Reverend C.W. Warbourton, a clergyman of the old sort and a genuinely pleasant fellow, took us on a guided tour of his parish. He owned a horse and trap and drove the mare with an assured crack of the whip.

That evening, as the sun set low over Balcombe and yet another train thundered through on the main line, we took a leisurely stroll in the churchyard. The parson, I observed, had a troubled look about him.

'They,' he surmised, taking out his gold repeater and checking the time, 'will be starting up soon.' He was referring to the local coven of witches whom he suspected were overseen by the landlord of The Horse and Hounds, a warlock by the name of Spencer. He surveyed the surrounding woodland with a trained eye. 'You will note, Mr Holmes and Doctor Watson, the cluster of trees upon the hill.

That is where the Sabbat shall take place – Cannonbury Ring.'

'May I make a plan of the graves?' asked Keeble, unfolding a large sheet of artist's paper and placing it flat against one of the tombs. 'I must position my legion of cameras – quite a lengthy procedure setting up these wires and tripods I'm afraid. Mr Holmes, Doctor Watson, would you care to assist?

'Certainly Lance,' said I, rolling up my sleeves. I returned to the station cart to help heave the gear. Holmes seemed more reluctant to exert himself.

'Lord protect us,' the parson said, invoking the Christian sign of the cross with a wide sweep of his arm. 'I have my library of religious books and tracts to consider. Those works of the mystic Saint John of Cupertino, the great thinkers and logicians, de Caspen, Valtelliana, the Dominican monk Gorres. We, gentlemen, must prepare ourselves for a paranormal onslaught of forces more evil than any of us dare contemplate. We meet for a light supper on the hour. I trust you will find plenty to amuse yourselves until then.'

After partaking of a light supper of beef broth, boiled fowl, roast suckling pig, a mixed salad and a generous helping of sherry trifle, we retired to the parson's book-lined study and enjoyed brandy and cigars.

From our comfortable armchairs we surveyed the trim little churchyard and indeed the simple church itself, through the French windows. There was a bright full moon and the sky was clear and dotted with a cluster of stars.

'What a lovely night,' I remember saying, taking a sip of excellent Napoleon brandy. My colleague could only agree.

'There is such a serene tranquillity abroad in Balcombe tonight,' he remarked, though somewhat sarcastically.

'A dreadful night.' The parson spoke in direct contrast. 'A night of evil, mark my words, Mr Holmes. Hallo, already a strange green light has appeared above one of the graves. It seems to hover there like a glow-worm.'

Keeble got up and positioned himself behind one of the box cameras over by the window. The elderly cleric leapt up from his leather club chair and went over to the window.

'Minor phenomenon, a will-o'-the-wisp, perhaps,' he muttered absently.

'Well, it's growing larger,' said Holmes with a bored look.

'The ball of light has swollen to the size of a football,' said I incredulously. 'It's expanding as we speak.'

A flash bulb exploded. The parson reached for his opera glasses.

'By Jove gentlemen, this is no mere will-o'-the-wisp after all,' he ejaculated. 'Oval in shape, a type of translucent bubble.'

'A giant egg.'

'Yes, that's a very apt description, Doctor Watson.'

The parson then went on to explain the phenomenon. 'This undoubtedly belongs to the

witches' pharmacopoeia. Their Sabbat on the hill
at Cannonbury Ring shall soon culminate in
unhallowed feats of necromancy. Spencer the warlock
has initiated a diabolical agency to conjure the dead
from their graves. It is much worse than I ever
envisaged. We are about to witness in Balcombe an
unholy procession of the shrouds.'

'Procession of the shrouds!' I repeated nervously.
'What – the walking dead?'

'The horror horn, the angels' trumpet, I must
fetch it from its case, there is not much time,' said
he.

Thus abandoning his vigil the parson bounded
out of the study.

'I hope I can catch some of these peculiar
fluctuations of light on the negative plates.' Young
Keeble pointed to the row of cameras he had placed
strategically outside in the churchyard, operated by
switches from inside the study.

I observed that the translucent egg hovering over
a grave had begun to grow long, writhing tentacles
of light that appeared to be searching out certain
unmarked plots on the north side.

'Unmarked graves,' said I.

'Where are usually buried suicides and felons,'
noted Holmes, watching proceedings with a
jaundiced eye, for I knew he believed us to have
been duped by a member of the Magic Circle, and
strongly suspected the Reverend C.W. Warbourton
was a master illusionist capable of using light and
mirrors to great effect.

'Indeed,' said an excited Keeble. 'The graves of
paupers and the unbaptised are usually to be found

on the north side of English churchyards. Come over here and look at this Doctor Watson.'

I shifted my position and was amazed to see the egg-shaped pod undergoing a rapid transformation, the fluidic matter changing shape inside.

'Holmes, there's some sort of figure materialising. It's got its arms outstretched. It's a sort of hooded monk.'

'Really,' said Holmes, sitting smoking his pipe, watching from his armchair, unfazed.

Suddenly we saw the parson scamper along the churchyard path by the yew hedge and, with his queer trumpet, leap up on top of a large tomb.

'Be gone thou blasphemous and perverse abomination of magicians whose sorceries I shall not permit to disturb the quiet of the grave!' he shouted, shielding his face from the glare of the green, palpitating light filling every space between the graves.

The spectral, hooded figure slowly rose and turned to face its antagonist, seemingly encased by the sinister protoplasmic egg. Its eerie glow shone the more intensely. The monkish, cowled entity pointed one of its long, bony fingers directly at the parson.

'Look out!' I cried from behind the glass pane, watching helplessly. I was expecting a deathly green ray to shoot out from the outstretched finger, but by now the parson had raised the horror horn to his lips and blew hard and long. The noise was awesome, a deep basso drone that filled the charged atmosphere, making the very ethers vibrate.

The evil entity sent by the warlock Spencer at the height of the Sabbat seemed to shiver and pulsate, the creature exploding back into the vortex from whence it had come. The danger was over and the churchyard settled back once more to normality. The parson held the trumpet above his head triumphantly and yelled so all might hear.

'Verily the evil is passed! My flock of peaceful Christian sleepers shall not be violated by Satan and his minions. Beelzebub hath departed to his hellish furnace house empty-handed!'

Holmes, in a state of heightened curiosity, a positive fever of speculation, rushed out of the house and began a systematic search of the vicinity, seeking a flaw with his magnifying lens, a logical explanation for what had just occurred. I knew he wished to prove beyond a shadow of a doubt that the Reverend C.W. Warbourton was a clever illusionist, a member of the Magic Circle, a master magician who had set the whole thing up using the latest trickery, but it was to no avail. For all that he discovered in the end was a scorch mark upon one of the graves as though the ground thereabouts had been subjected to intense heat.

The reader's sympathy however should not rest solely with my companion, who for once could not solve the mystery, but rather poor Lance Keeble, for the young amateur photographer discovered in the dark room that he had garnered not one useful image on his negative plates, which had suffered over-exposure. There was nothing to record that dramatic night in Balcombe.

Are ghosts or entities merely vestiges of a decaying personality or thought complex, triggered, perhaps by the witches' Sabbat taking place at a secret location in the parish? F. W. H. Myers, the respected author and expert upon psychical matters, suggested this:

> When two or three persons see what seems to be the same phantom in the same place and at the same time, does that mean that a special part of time and space is somehow modified? Or, does it mean that a mental impression conveyed by the distant agent – the phantom begetter to one of the percipients is reflected telepathically from one mind to the other?

Whatever the phantasmagorical impressions Holmes and myself received that night at Balcombe have remained a tantalising conundrum ever since.

10

Murder on the Croydon Suburban Railway

Changeable weather is no unusual occurrence in November, and so it was from the bay window of our modest bachelor apartments in Baker Street upon a day of extremes – sharp frost and thick fog in the early morning followed by strong gusts of wind and hail – we watched, with amused interest, a cab arrive outside our lodgings and a young Inspector of Police, well known to us, step out onto the wet pavement, only to almost instantly lose his bowler, the wind sending it scuttling across the road. Were it not for an energetic sprint he should never have retrieved his hat from over by the newspaper vendor's pitch.

Not long after, we received a knock at the door to our rooms.

'Why, Stanley Hopkins,' said Holmes, slinging his copy of the *Telegraph* aside and reaching for his oily black clay from the convivial pipe rack. 'What brings you here on such a foul and overcast morning? You must be chilled to the bone, man! Watson, pour our budding Scotland Yarder a warming cup of coffee.'

The florid-faced detective, fresh from his exertions, removed his grey bowler and tweed overcoat and stood in front of the fireguard warming himself, glad to be indoors and out of the bitter wind.

'Well, Mr Holmes, it's a little puzzle of matrimony, wedding bells if you will, gone dreadfully sour.'

Holmes struck a match to his pipe and frowned.

'Dear me,' said he glumly. 'Hopkins, I am disappointed in you. Dull, dull, dull. I was expecting better from an ambitious Scotland Yarder such as yourself. You'll not go far in the force spying on illicit bedroom antics at a Brighton boarding house, I can assure you.'

The detective grimaced.

'Hold your horses, Mr Holmes, please allow me to finish. The reason I have called at your rooms this morning is to tell you that there has been a murder in South Norwood near Croydon. The details are bound to be of interest to you and I shall require both yourself and Doctor Watson to accompany me to the scene of crime.'

'You've been out and about then, Hopkins,' said I, handing him his cup and returning to my usual armchair, glad to note that my companion was positively straining at the leash, so delighted was he that a case of such singular merit was at hand, for a murder offered endless possibilities to test his considerable wits against a criminal adversary.

'Quite so, Doctor Watson. I should summarise my morning's expedition to South Norwood thus. At approximately four thirty this morning, a cleaner working through the carriages at the Selhurst depot discovered a body lying prone in one of the compartments. It was a naked young man dressed only in a cream, satin bridal gown and veil, who had been stabbed through the heart by a long sharp implement such as a knitting needle.'

'Considerable strength should be required to perform such a task,' said my colleague.

'My feelings exactly, Mr Holmes. The entry wound was merely a tiny hole and little blood was evident due to internal bleeding, so the police surgeon in attendance tells me.'

'Just the one single blow to the heart? No other injuries?' I asked.

'None.'

'Capital, we can therefore assume the young man was murdered at another location, and the body later placed in the compartment. Hallo, is that the time already? Half past eight; there is, I believe, a train that runs upon the hour calling at Tulse Hill, Norbury, Thornton Heath and Selhurst from London Bridge. Finish your coffee, Inspector.'

My esteemed companion leapt up from his chair and hurried over to the door of our front sitting-room.

'Mrs Hudson, Mrs Hudson!' he yelled. 'Summon a cab if you will. We have but half an hour to cross London and catch a suburban train. By Jove, Watson, it's an umbrella day! That heavy, lowering cloud over the city portends the very worst of inclement weather.'

We took the stopping service from London Bridge and, against a dun and steely grey sky, arrived at Selhurst at around ten. An earlier fine drizzle had formed into a sleety downpour and, as our train departed, rusty ditch water driven by the strong gusting wind swished across the tracks.

Inspector Stanly Hopkins, accompanied by a senior railway employee, Mr Croft, led our party across the converging metals to a siding, where a row of some twelve coaches belonging to the Croydon Suburban Railway Company awaited cleaning. Thence, brandishing our umbrellas to fend off the worst of the wind and cold biting rain gusting about the depot, we walked along beside the track for quite a way until we reached a set of steps propped up against a non-smoking, second-class compartment guarded on the ground by a pair of stout policemen wearing wet weather capes, looking to all intents and purposes like the proverbial drowned rats.

Following Holmes's ardent stride, climbing the steps into the compartment, I quickly perceived we were in the presence of death, for the wide-open carriage door revealed the lifeless body within, a person rudely sprawled across one of the cloth-covered seats resembling an oversized porcelain doll.

'We have no idea who this fellow is, Mr Holmes,' said Stanley Hopkins sadly. 'No identification whatsoever. No proper clothes to speak of except this hideous bridal apparel. Spooked the life out of me he did, when I first saw him lying there, poor devil.'

'Stabbed through the heart,' said Mr Croft, leaning forward to gloat upon the corpse.

'By a meat skewer, or a sharpened knitting needle. You're correct, Hopkins, this is no shallow wound caused by, say, a hat pin. My dear Watson, pray what are your observations so far?'

'Well, Holmes,' said I, shoving Mr Croft aside to

study the specimen closely. 'I should concur that, judging by the point of entry, this young man died from a precise punching blow to the heart, possibly piercing the aortic valve, causing considerable internal bleeding.'

'Indeed,' said Holmes, 'there's so little blood about. Even the flouncy wedding gown possesses only an innocuous stain, yet the strength required to push the skewer or needle home must have been considerable.'

'We are looking for a man of some physical strength then, a navvy or a wheel tapper, someone working on the railways?' asked young Inspector Hopkins.

'Quite possibly,' answered my companion, taking out a pair of metal tweezers from his inner pocket and plucking a long, golden hair from the lacy bridal veil. He briefly held it up to the poor winter's light of an overcast day before depositing the hair in a convenient envelope he specially carried.

'Can't we make him decent?' said I, appalled by the way his naked, pale flesh was only partly concealed from view.

'Stretcher, blankets!' shouted the detective. 'Make it sharp, lads, I think we're done here now.'

'A moment if you please, Hopkins.' Holmes had spied yet another lengthy strand of golden blonde hair, this time on the cream material of the bridal gown itself. Once the hair was bagged into the envelope he indicated that we should leave. 'The train which is in your depot, Mr Croft, what time was it shunted in?'

'A late-night stopping service from London Bridge,

sir, terminating at Norwood Junction. The eleven fifty-nine. The carriages would have been deposited at the siding around one-twenty, but the cleaners did not begin their duties until a quarter past four.'

'You excel yourself, Mr Croft. Might I confirm that the two suburban stations along the line from here are Thornton Heath and Norbury?'

'Just so, sir, the late service train would have called at those same stops last night.'

'I am indebted to you, Mr Croft. Come Watson. Inspector Hopkins, the next train for Norwood Junction is in an hour – is there a quicker way?'

'Norwood, sir? A number 23 omnibus'll take you there in fifteen minutes. If you walk up Selhurst Road, twenty or so.'

'Well, at least the rain has stopped for a brief interlude, but it's still blowing and fearfully cold in this suburban precinct of south London. I think a brisk trudge is in order. The fresh air and exercise will do us the power of good, eh, Watson?'

At the brow of Upper Selhurst Road the loud and persistent ring of a bicycle bell was our first indication that a diligent member of the local force was close behind. On being informed of our route he had cycled at a hectic pace along Selhust Road and barely managed to catch us on the Rise.

A hurried conversation took place between the out-of-breath local officer and his superior, Inspector Stanley Hopkins of the Yard. Thereafter, the constable was dismissed on his bike and the detective informed us of certain fresh developments.

'Well I'm blowed,' said he, leaning against a pillar

box while delivery carts and cabs and wagons drove by. 'The Transport Police have arrested a railway vagrant by the name of Chester, who was tented up along the embankment between Thornton Heath and Norbury. About to move him on, a sergeant cleverly observed a pile of fairly newish clothes amongst his belongings. One worsted jacket, a pair of trousers, lambskin overcoat, felt hat and a pair of recently heeled size nine and a half brogues, scarf and woollen gloves. The lot purchased from Hewitts Emporium in Croydon.'

'The officer is to be commended, my dear fellow, but what is that you have clasped so fervently in your hand, Inspector?'

'No wallet was found when the pockets were checked, only a W.H. Smith receipt for 3/6d.'

Holmes snatched the handwritten docket and examined it carefully. 'A mass of jumbled numbers that mean little to the purchaser or ourselves. However, a W.H. Smith's trade kiosk is surely on hand along the platform of Norwood Junction station. You were about to say something, Hopkins?'

'Mr Holmes, it is surely not lost on yourself or Doctor Watson that these clothes found in the tramp's tent could belong to our naked man in the train carriage?'

'It had crossed my mind, certainly.'

'And thus, the person who carried out this murder could conceivably be Chester?'

'Unlikely, indeed highly improbable,' remarked my companion, as we each of us unfurled our umbrellas, for it had started to rain again.

'It's all rather queer, this bridal-inspired slaying.

It reeks of sophistication, Inspector. Tell me, why on earth should a lowly tramp go to the bother of dressing up a corpse in a wedding gown, a clean and neatly pressed garment at that? If only we could penetrate the problem further. By all means keep Chester in custody but I fear the real murderer is still at large in south London. The W.H. Smith's receipt for 3/6d offers us a superior lead, I believe.'

We continued our walk along Selhurst Road to the High Street, and upon reaching the clock tower we advanced swiftly to Norwood Junction station.

On the down platform was situated the familiar W.H. Smith kiosk. A young lad was serving at the hatch but he was evidently a trainee for he lacked the necessary experience to deal with difficult requests from the customer.

Holmes leaned on his cane and passed him the crumpled piece of paper.

'Wot's that then?'

'A receipt for 3/6d. I wish to ascertain the place it was issued and also, if possible, a description of the item purchased.'

'Lummy, sir, that's a most unusual request I'm sure. After all, it's only a smidgeon of old paper, barely legible.'

'We are aware of that,' said Stanley Hopkins, losing patience and on the precipice of losing his temper. 'Mr Holmes here is a consulting detective and I represent Scotland Yard. There has, I'm sorry to say, been a murder.'

'Murder. Blimey!'

'Ah, move aside Squires,' said an older, more confident man, assuming control of the situation.

'Now gents, what do we have here? A receipt? My name's Barlow, I'm the vendor.'

The fellow licked his lips and put on a pair of spectacles, screwing up his eyes before making a minute study of the details listed on the receipt.

'Forty-two denotes London Bridge station, number four our large kiosk situated on the main concourse. You may perchance have visited there.'

'Why of course,' exclaimed Holmes. 'I often purchase my newspapers at the stand when visiting the city.'

'Naturally. Now the signature A.C. refers to Alf Crabtree, an assistant manager. H/B 22H is in fact, now let me just check this list in front of me, ah, a hardback volume, the latest Hilda Tullow romance novel, *The Scarecrow Bride*, price 3/6d. Doing very nicely sales wise, been out for a couple of weeks now. That do yer?'

'May I congratulate you, Mr Barlow, on running a first-rate kiosk, and also might I commend W.H. Smith for its logistical and time-saving method of accountancy. Bravo.'

'We does our best to please the customer,' said he, becoming overly puffed up.

'Might I purchase a copy of *The Scarecrow Bride*, though the author, I fear, quite eludes me?'

'Excuse me, sir, Hilda Tullow is something of a local celebrity, opening garden fetes, attending town hall 'do's', giving talks at the church hall in South Norwood. We stock all four of her books in our popular reading section.'

'Local celebrity, you say?' said I.

'Yes, she lives along Tennyson Road. A nicer person

171

it would be hard to meet. Does tireless work for the south London waifs and strays clubs, I believe. Lovely lookin' an' all. Ha ha. That'll be 3/6d, sir. Would you like me to wrap the book up for you?'

'No, leave it as it is please.'

'Well, Holmes,' said I, whilst we retraced our steps to Norwood High Street, once more encountering the clock tower on our travels. 'According to the *Times* review, Hilda Tullow writes in the style of Emily Brontë, else Mrs Gaskell.'

'The sleeve notes are more than adequate to form a hypothesis, thank you, Watson. Pray digest the same if you will, and you also, Hopkins, observing in particular the garish cover picture of a bridal gown.'

We proceeded along the main thoroughfare until we came to Tennyson Road, a turning to our left. We had little trouble in locating the popular author's pretty detached villa built of red brick and stucco, two storeys, plus attic, situated in a high-class residential area of South Norwood.

Holmes tugged the bell pull and a distinct clanging could be heard from within. A shadow loomed large in the frosted glass, whereupon a bustling, fussy maid opened the front door.

We were standing beneath the arched porch about to explain our business, when a petite blonde lady, presumably the author, appeared in the hallway. What a stunningly beautiful profile she possessed as she glanced coquettishly in the gilt mirror, smoothing down her skirts. Her hair was tied in a delightful little topknot and she was blessed with all the fine, noble-womanly qualities that men find impossible to ignore.

Holmes immediately sprung into action, for he was a first-rate actor and could pull off any part required.

'Might I bother you for an autograph? I dare say a signed photo would be too much to ask?' My companion removed his hat and held it penitently in hand. 'I should explain, madam, we are a group of Croydon bachelors, slavishly devoted to the works of Hilda Tullow. Your latest creation, *The Scarecrow Bride*, is a book Emily Brontë herself would have been proud to write. I found myself literally in tears, Miss Tullow, in tears over the way the mill girl Flo' dies so early on in the story, having been murdered so horribly upon the eve of her wedding to Captain Carson.'

'Why, you flatter me, Mister-?'

'Mr Medley from south Croydon.'

'Well, Mr Medley and you too, gentlemen, by all means come inside. It looks like more rain unfortunately. That's it, put your umbrellas and wet things on the hall stand. My secretary, Miss Carruthers, is presently in her office and I am sure will furnish you with an autographed photo. You will forgive me but I must return to my writing.'

'Thank you, thank you and thank you again, Miss Tullow,' grovelled Holmes, playing the part of the besotted admirer to a tee in a final rapturous, if entirely false, display of sentiment as we stepped into the house and were led along the hall to the secretary's office.

'A signed photograph, if you please, Miss Carruthers,' she called out, ushering us into the book-lined sanctuary before leaving us alone with the formidable woman seated behind a vast imposing oak desk, cluttered with piles of unread manuscripts and unopened correspondence, smoking a large briar pipe.

While young Hopkins and I gazed around the smoky, tobacco-filled room, pretending to be overwhelmed admirers of Miss Tullow the novelist, my companion calmly took out his own pipe and began the ritual of filling it with tobacco from a pouch, which interested the author's secretary greatly.

'Ha, what d'ya smoke that old rope for? Listen, my tobacconist in Burlington Arcade makes me up a nice Hollanders mixture. Player's Uncut is surely preferable to Sailor's shag.'

'Indeed, Miss Carruthers. Might I introduce myself? I am Sherlock Holmes and this is my companion, Doctor Watson. Mr Stanley Hopkins is the third interested party.'

'Glad to meet you, I'm sure.' She was a short stocky woman with a mannish face, possessing an alarming military short back and sides. Her clothes were equally unconventional, purchased from a gentleman's outfitters: tweedy jacket, plus-fours and a fine pair of leather hunting boots. She gave each of us a firm handshake but regarded us warily. Smoking her pipe, she resumed her seat, folded her arms and frowned at us intently.

'What can I do for you gentlemen? Are you from the press looking for an inside story?'

'*The Scarecrow Bride,* the prominent jacket illustration showing a wedding gown...'

'What of it? Hank Streeter is the creative artist. He's done all Hilda's books. *Lovers' Tryst at Darnsley*

Hall, Ponsonby-Rake of the Fifth Hussars, Mr Dashwood of Denby Fell. Elder and Co., the publishers, swear by him. Cover art shifts books. In Hilda Tullow's case a million and a half copies and still counting.'

'Reading the copious sleeve notes, it emerges a bridal gown is draped over a turnip-headed scarecrow, left on the grave of Flo', a mill girl who has been murdered on the eve of her wedding by a jealous parson by the name of – what was it?'

'The Reverend Elijah.'

'Just so, who ends up becoming a bishop, is never found out but later, full of remorse, flings himself from the spire of a church in Haworth.'

'The plot's not one of Miss Tullow's strongest, but she creates superb atmosphere. Flo' wandering the moors, for example, destitute and starving until she meets quite by chance this Captain Carson character, the love of her life. As a popular author she can produce a thousand-page "potboiler" in six months flat. That's why the publishers love her. Mind you, it can take an age to type them up.'

'Good gracious, is that a wild pheasant I see running amok in your garden? Miss Tullow shall surely need to be notified,' said Holmes, an astonished look on his face.

'What the Dickens?'

The curious secretary, sucking on the stem of her pipe noisily, got up from behind her desk, stomped over to the French windows and peered anxiously outside to locate the errant bird, which of course was non-existent, allowing Holmes, while her back was turned, to remove a letter from the spike on her desk which, unbeknown to her, he pocketed for future reference. Not to be outdone, Inspector Stanley Hopkins snatched a Croydon Literary Circle leaflet from a partly open drawer.

'I like my hunting,' she said at length, more to herself than us. 'Horse and hounds. Got a fine young gelding, Golden Fancy, good for the chase, bounding over hedges and fences, eh?' She appeared to me overly boastful, knowing full well that the polite gentlemen callers before her were unlikely to take part in field sports, for riding a hunter at a good gallop required a steely nerve and unremitting concentration, a frisson of danger always present.

'That wily old pheasant you saw must have gone to ground behind the fence. I might bag it for the pot later.'

'You keep firearms on the premises?' remarked the Inspector incredulously, forgetting he was meant to be acting the civilian.

'You sound like a ruddy policeman. Course I keep firearms on the premises. I own a couple of first-rate Purdeys – guns inherited from my father, engraved silver stocks, the lot, beautiful things. Y'know, I often escort Hilda to country-house weekends, but she's a squeamish filly, wouldn't dare take part in the shoot.'

'Really. I hear a young man's been murdered, Miss Carruthers, found naked in a train carriage wearing only a wedding dress, a bridal gown of cream satin,' remarked my companion, relighting his own pipe. 'At Selhurst, it's only down the road from here.'

'You're surely not trying to link a work of pure fiction with some Soho low-life, who probably got what he deserved. Coincidence that's all.'

'You appear rather quick off the mark, Miss Carruthers. Does not a young man murdered and left alone in such an exposed and vulnerable condition in a railway carriage evoke some vestige of sympathy?'

'Utter rot. Listen here, gents, go to Soho, there's a club, "The Wages of Sin" in Berwick Street, that'll open your eyes a bit.'

The secretary continued smoking her pipe, no doubt aware of our intense displeasure at her crass remarks.

'That's a damnably trite allegation,' said I. 'What possible evidence have you linking this dead chap in the compartment with a sordid West End club?'

'Calm yourself, dear boy,' directed Holmes. 'The police may yet be forced to follow that exact same line of enquiry. Miss Carruthers is most perceptive. My dear lady, we have taken up enough of your valuable time. Our conversation has been most pleasant and enlightening. Oh, and the best of luck with bagging that old rogue pheasant. Give him a blast of number twelve shot for me.'

'Delighted to meet you, sir. Here's the autographed picture you requested.' She once more shook us firmly by the hand. 'And don't forget what I told ya! Player's Uncut or my tobacconist W.W. Purnell's along Burlington Arcade could rustle you up a decent Hollander mixture. Anything but that ropey old shag. Good day gentlemen, I see it's started to rain again.'

We took a brisk walk up by the Goat House Bridge, where we then enjoyed a good lunch at a local

Italian restaurant. Over the beef risotto cooked and served by Mama Chianto, a generously bosomed Italian matriarch whose family ran the place, my esteemed companion put aside his plate and unfolded the letter he had earlier secreted upon his person before leaving the author's house. He read it out loud to us.

Dear Miss Tullow,
It has now been over six months since I requested the return of my manuscript 'Miss Elisa of Marsdon Hall.' The MS, including my heartfelt letter praising your work and begging only a morsel, a crumb of your kindness to glance over my writing and perhaps offer constructive criticism, else suggest a publisher, or better still a writer's agent, remains unanswered. Is it a habit of yours to ignore the less fortunate unpublished writer? Has all the money and fame (you must surely have accrued substantial royalties since the publication of Lovers' Tryst at Darnsley Hall*!) turned your head?*
You have quite tried my patience and I have in mind a way of making your life a misery. Your wealth and fame will not protect you from my wrath. I think I shall become your shadow unto the end.
Yours
Cecily Finch

'By Jove, Watson, this seems clear enough. A popular novelist, like the busy publisher and literary agent, will receive countless manuscripts every week, many of them sent from hopeful aspirants, unpublished writers forgetting to include return postage, and this is the result, for they cannot possibly all be read. The task should be far too time-consuming. What have you got there, Hopkins?'

'The Croydon Literary Circle's agenda for last night's meeting, a talk from the novelist Miss Tullow, on the writing of a successful romance. The biographer T.O. Wills speaks of his latest book concerning Gladstone. Mrs Hartnell, herself an author of mysteries, presents a writer's workshop.'

'Last night you say – whereabouts?'

'Thornton Heath. The Croydon Literary Circle meets once a month at 24 Victoria Terrace, the home of the Chairwoman, Mrs Edith Hartnell.'

'Capital. Let's finish our meal and catch the next train to Thornton Heath. I should very much like to talk with the porter and find out if he remembers anything out of the ordinary concerning the late-night stopping service from London Bridge. We shall also pay a call to this Mrs Hartnell. The Croydon Literary Circle interests me.'

That same afternoon we found ourselves ensconced upon the Croydon Suburban Railway. The rain persisted until evening, most of southern England caught in a deluge.

'Well, that secretary was a spirited woman,' said I. 'Such a contrast to Miss Tullow, whom I personally found charming and highly approachable despite her considerable fame.'

'Agreed,' said Hopkins, gazing at the rain-spotted compartment window as our train pulled into Thornton Heath. 'A lovely lady.'

'I suspect Miss Carruthers is probably rather shy and timid beneath that blustering, bullish exterior. She nonetheless proved most helpful,' said Holmes.

'Helpful? I should have said she was a downright hindrance to our enquiry. I've never met a more brash and insensitive individual in my life,' I asserted.

We alighted at the station and paused to watch our train trundle off down the line to Norbury. A wetter, more overcast and gloomy day it would be hard to imagine. The platform was covered in a mass of puddles, the end being completely water-logged, and, the station guttering was overflowing.

Inspector Stanley Hopkins duly informed the elderly porter, Mr Swinton, that we were on police business regarding the naked body of a young man discovered in a train compartment wearing a lady's bridal gown. The porter was scathing.

'I sees 'em.' He spoke angrily. 'Low life from them seedy London clubs, turfed out late at night I expect. Abnormal dressing up like a fairy in a frock, wearin' full make-up was 'e? Deserved to die. Scum of the earth them queer types.'

'There's nothing remotely that links this young man to Soho nightclubs,' said I, infuriated by the old fellow's blatantly biased attitude. 'You're a bigot. Try travelling around the world with the army, you'll soon learn to appreciate others' cultural differences.'

'Bigot, am I? Well, someone done us an honest turn last night, done the right thing. I'd do the same meself. Well, I wouldn't commit murder, you understand, just rough 'im up a bit. Anyhow gents, come into the parcels office and I'll make yer a nice mug o' tea. This bloomin' rain seems set to last.'

'Most kind of you, Mr Swinton,' said Holmes, resisting the urge to knock him over the head with his cane. 'You were presumably on duty when the late service from London Bridge arrived. Were there many passengers awaiting to board the train at Thornton Heath last night?'

'Just the two, sir, couple of drunks, one of 'em built like a hippo. Short and stocky wearing a tweed cap and woolly scarf, the other gentleman so far gone he were virtually insensible, being carried along the platform supported by his companion. They both of 'em slumped into the carriage an' I slammed the door behind 'em.'

'No other persons were waiting for the train?'

'No, the late service is generally fairly empty, goes on to Norwood then the carriages gets reversed by a shunter into the depot for cleaning. You can 'ear the goods yard working through the night if you live round Selhurst way. The late stopping service takes on bundles of early morning papers and sacks of mail deposited in the guard's van but passengers at that time of night are generally few and far between.'

Mrs Hartnell's home in Thornton Heath, number 24 Victoria Terrace, was a neat, prim little two-storey house built of Gault brick with a pedimented doorway upon a scroll bracket. I was, like young Hopkins, astonished when Holmes asked her a question neither of us had been expecting. I recall it was still raining heavily and I was drenched through.

The lady, the Chairwoman of the Croydon Literary Circle, greeted us on the porch with folded arms and a quizzical expression upon her chubby features.

'What can I do for you, gentlemen?'

'Mrs Hartnell, my name is Sherlock Holmes and this is my colleague, Doctor Watson. I am a consulting detective from London and this is Inspector Stanley Hopkins from Scotland Yard. We are investigating a murder in which a young man was found naked in a railway carriage at Selhurst depot.'

'Oh, how exciting!' she trilled.

'The corpse of a young man, I should emphasise,' said Holmes with some amusement, 'wearing only a bridal gown. Might I trouble you to venture upstairs to your bedroom and tell me if your own pristine wedding dress – kept, I am sure, always clean and perfectly ironed at the back of the wardrobe in mothballs – is still there?'

We waited hesitantly while a light came on upstairs and we were left shivering beneath our dripping umbrellas. The light in the upstairs window was extinguished once more and not long after a worried-looking Mrs Hartnell came back downstairs.

'How ... how did you know it was not there, Mr Holmes? I remember I packed it away last month after giving it a good iron. My bridal gown is missing from my wardrobe.'

'The colour is cream, the material satin and lace, floral motifs sewn onto the hem.'

'The very same. You're not going to tell me the bridal garment worn by this poor dead man is mine? How could it have possibly ended up there?'

'If we might bother you for a cup of tea, Mrs

Hartnell, I shall endeavour to explain. The rain and wind, you know, hasn't let up all day.' Never was a broader hint given.

'Oh, I'm so sorry, gentlemen. You look soaked. Here, take off your wet things and I shall make us all a nice pot of tea. My husband is working late at his office. He commutes every day to the city of course.'

I confess the revelation concerning the wedding gown had left me reeling. Holmes had once more applied his logical reasoning to solving an outstanding problem concerning the case. Now we had our wedding gown, what of the murderer?

Mrs Hartnell fussed over us and brought in a tray of tea things from the kitchen. Holmes had meanwhile been prowling about on all fours examining the lino with his magnifying lens, and was the last to take his chair.

'Milk and sugar, gentlemen? Help yourselves. The biscuits are in the tin.'

'Well, Mrs Hartnell, I think I owe you an explanation. The wedding gown was in fact stolen by one of your Croydon Literary Circle who met here last night. You may recall the author Hilda Tullow employs an ebullient secretary, Miss Carruthers, who will of course accompany her to such literary gatherings. It was she and she alone who stole your bridal gown. She must have crept upstairs while the meeting was in progress, eager to ferret around your wardrobe and obtain such a garment, for it would play a part in the murderous scheme she had devised and was about to implement. It will not surprise you to learn, my dear Watson, that Cecily Finch, the writer of the threatening letter, is merely an alias, a pseudonym for the naked gentleman found murdered in the train compartment.'

'My dear fellow,' I ejaculated, 'what masterly reasoning, I must congratulate you most profoundly on your deductions. But why should Miss Carruthers choose to murder this man in the first place? Because of a few nasty letters full of frustration and longing for the life of a successful author? Surely not.'

'Alas, he was primarily a determined and tenacious stalker, Watson. The letter, you will recall, made mention of "I think I shall become your shadow unto the very end". Prophetic as it turned out. Consider if you will, Hopkins, the misery caused by such detestable behaviour directed solely at a popular and attractive young woman, his only mistake being that he failed to take account of the formidable Miss Carruthers, a devoted secretary, a long-time friend. She would not hesitate in pitting her own strengths, those of a keen huntswoman, a first-rate bagger of fowls, snipe and partridge, a lover of field sports, of the chase, dispatching the fox with consummate skill, against what she correctly perceived to be an open threat against her mistress's wellbeing by a usurper, a man who thought he could intimidate a popular romantic author by following her from church on a Sunday, lurking in shop doorways, shadowing her every move until he chose to strike. In short, a pathetic madman.'

'Excuse me interrupting, Mr Holmes, but I remember last night Miss Carruthers seemed unusually ill at ease the entire evening, occasionally glancing tentatively out of the living-room window at the pavement lamp outside, her whole being tense and speculative. I implored the dear old thing to sit down and relax, smoke her pipe, but she simply shrugged it off.'

'She knew instinctively that the stalker was close by, possibly watching the house from that clump of woods across the road. I believe that was where he was killed, stabbed with a meat skewer. If only Miss Tullow had spoken of this more publicly, not been afraid to speak her mind to the police, all of this could have been averted and this aggrieved, unpublished author taken into custody and discreetly removed to a lunatic asylum before he could cause further harm.'

'A stalker is a mean piece of work, Mr Holmes, but you are correct – Miss Carruthers should never have taken the law into her own hands. It's the black cap for her if the jury judges her guilty, which it surely will.'

'Be that as it may, I propose the actual crime was perpetrated in the woods across the road, the fox dispatched some time after the writers' circle finished its meeting and dispersed.'

'But how on earth did the body end up on a railway siding?' said I, at a complete loss.

'You recall, my dear fellow, the pair of drunks the porter Mr Swinton mentioned stumbling along the platform before boarding the train at Thornton Heath? Well, that same station is just up the road from here.'

'How damnably convenient,' said Inspector Hopkins, biting on another biscuit. 'A clever deception, dragging the dead fellow along, pretending him to be legless and the worse for drink, bundling him into the train compartment before dressing him up in Mrs Hartnell's wedding gown.'

'Incidentally, the long golden hairs I removed from the gown with a pair of tweezers came from your golden retriever, Mrs Hartnell, for Miss Carruthers accidentally dropped the bridal dress on the kitchen floor when she crept out through the back door. The close proximity of the dog basket provides us with a useful clue to the movements of the author's secretary prior to her crossing the road undetected and dealing with the stalker for the final time.'

'Well, there's nothing else for it, we must arrest the lady in question,' said Hopkins ruefully.

Although it pains me to do so, I shall now do my best to recount the tragic circumstances that unfolded in South Norwood upon that cold and bitter windswept November night in 1894. The passage of time has not dimmed my perception of events. I recall still our hansom rattling along a murky, misty Selhurst Road, its bell tinkling, our primary concern being for Miss Tullow's physical safety and that of her loyal domestics. I do not use the words 'armed and dangerous' lightly, for you may recall Miss Carruthers owned a very rare and expensive pair of Purdey shotguns and knew how to use them to great effect when shooting game birds. Inspector Stanley Hopkins, with the full cooperation of the local force, was about to sanction an arrest.

'I'll not be bowed by Miss Carruthers,' he said,

'nor her filthy briar pipe.' Inspector Hopkins patted his inner jacket pocket where he normally kept his police-issue handgun.

'The plan is for you to grab her wrists, Doctor Watson, while I apply the cuffs, and Mr Holmes restrains her with his cane. To hesitate, Lord knows she could flatten us, she's built like a champion wrestler.'

'Her possession of firearms bothers me,' said I.

'Upon my word, Watson, we find ourselves in the thick of it all right. I shouldn't fancy looking down the twin barrels of a Purdey for anything,' remarked my companion, his thin, eager face aglow while smoking his oily black clay.

Our hansom trotted to a standstill outside number 27. It was dark and chilly, the lime trees thereabouts dripping wet.

'Miss Carruthers may yet prove a ruthless adversary, capable of escaping the clutches of the law. Ah, I observe your Black Maria is parked strategically lower down the road, well concealed by the shadow of the limes. How many additional officers have we, Inspector?'

'Dobson, the local man, has mustered a force of three part-time constables – totally inadequate. He is of the opinion Miss Carruthers will come quietly, offer no resistance. I begged to differ and wired Scotland Yard. The Black Maria they sent contains a further six burly officers – also a dog handler from the compound over at Kennington. A semi-starved bull terrier is a ferocious animal capable of bringing down a bullock when sufficiently riled, Mr Holmes.'

'Unfortunately they are also notoriously unreliable, and can turn on the wrong person at the drop of a hat. I should have preferred a mastiff, else a German Shepherd myself.'

We approached the vine-clad porch of the detached red brick villa and, heartbreakingly, it was the lovely Hilda who answered the door.

'Why, Mr Medley,' she smiled. 'How nice to see you again. I regret to inform you Croydon bachelors, this lady is for cocoa and bed. I had a long day of it writing the next chapter of my, as yet, untitled romance.'

'My dear madam,' said Holmes, reverting to the timid and wholly pathetic personality of Medley. 'A friend of mine is so desperate for a photograph – a picture of your lovely self.'

'All right. Annie!' she called out to her maid, 'fetch Kate here, will you? Is she in her office?'

'She's coming, ma'am,' I heard the domestic servant say. The stomp of hunting boots and a familiar manly laugh announced the audacious presence of the author's secretary, who came to the door wearing a heavy dressing gown and pyjamas, a well-smoked briar pipe clenched between her teeth.

'What's to do?' she said cheerfully, but then she realised something was up and her mood changed.

'You're under arrest for the murder of the recently identified Sydney Blackberry, a clerk from Croydon working for the Gas Board, who writes part-time under the pseudonym Cecily Finch. His body was discovered early this morning at Selhurst depot by a cleaner. What do you have to say?'

'Go to hell! So you were the damned police after all. What a lousy trick. Cowards, the lot of you.' Seizing the moment, my colleague Mr Sherlock Holmes leapt forward and gave her a whack with his trusty cane. I myself struggled to force her arms behind her back but it proved a wasted effort trying to restrain this great grizzly bear of a woman. Likewise, Inspector Stanley Hopkins clumsily failed to apply the cuffs properly and it was another fumbled opportunity lost.

Meanwhile, during the confusion, Miss Carruthers bounded back inside the house and a door slammed shut.

'Damn the woman, it's the back garden and over the fence, I dare say,' cursed the Scotland Yarder.

He blew his whistle and a loud, raucous barking could be heard, then a struggle taking place. The dog handler had done his job well and positioned himself and the bull terrier behind the garden shed, but to little avail, for loud shots could be heard as twin barrels discharged with terrible ferocity. There was a pitiful whine and then silence. The dog had been dealt with, perhaps its handler too.

Thereafter we heard footsteps running up the road.

'Follow her!' cried a local man, a detective I recognised by the name of Dobson, who was as incompetent as they come. 'She's headed towards Norwood High Street I think.'

'Oh, what's poor Kate got herself into now?' Hilda sobbed, pulling me closer to her so I was aware of her breath upon my ear. I could smell her exquisite rose-petal perfume.

'She's in very deep,' I said gravely, holding her in my arms to offer meagre comfort in her time of trial. 'Miss Carruthers may have been, in her own unique way, trying to protect you, but murdering somebody is not the correct way to go about it.'

'Shielding me from that awful stalker, the naked chap found on the train. Sydney Blackberry from Croydon, who pestered me so, followed me everywhere, making my life a misery, distracting me from my writing.'

'I fear that appears to be the case, Miss Tullow,' said I, accepting her proffered arm. 'Don't distress yourself further. Let's catch up with the others.'

I sheltered the poor, dear lady beneath my umbrella and together we advanced along the pavement. The rain appeared to have eased and the reflection of the street lamps' hazy orbs lined our route.

A Black Maria tore past, the hooves of the galloping horses clattering against the tarmacadam surface of the wet road. We could hear the distant shouts of police officers but, mercifully, no gun shots.

Once we emerged onto the High Street proper, beyond a group of shops, an incredible scene was taking place. The strangest sight greeted us for, like a jungle orang-utan desperate to avoid capture, Miss Carruthers was scaling the side of Norwood clock tower, a shotgun strapped across her shoulder. She clambered upwards towards the wrought iron clock face, digging her fingers into every available crevice of masonry, seeming to balance precariously upon every ledge, always with one purpose in mind: to reach the pinnacle, a steepled, arched roof bordered by ornamental railings, from where she could take aim and fire randomly on the crowd, many of them police officers anxious to arrest her, gathering beneath.

I and Holmes, together with Inspector Hopkins, having had previous experience in this type of stand-off, knew only too well the outcome. She would kill as many of the bystanders below as possible, before taking her own life.

'I've had enough of this,' said the Inspector, taking out his handgun, for he was not prepared to risk allowing the desperate woman to kill again. 'Mr Holmes, Doctor Watson, you will act as witnesses.'

'Assuredly, Inspector. Come man, hurry up and take aim, she's nearly reached the top and then we're all vulnerable, including you, Miss Tullow. Step into that shop doorway, my dear, if you value your life.'

'Isn't there another way?' she cried hopelessly, her pretty features awash with tears.

'There's no other way,' murmured Stanley Hopkins, calmly but resolutely squeezing the trigger of his revolver.

The first shot flew wide, grazing the clock tower's masonry, causing a fluffy deposit of dust. The second ricocheted against the wrought ironwork of the clock face with a metallic zinging sound. The third hit its intended target between the shoulder blades. Feeling a sense of revulsion, I gently placed my gloved hand over Hilda's worried eyes to thus, I hoped, spare her the agony of witnessing her friend's last moments.

I myself saw her devoted secretary of so many years tense briefly before losing her grip and falling backwards, tumbling off the clock tower from a great height, thereafter landing with a sickening thud upon the pavement.

As the drizzle started to fall in the dim mustard glow cast by one of the street lamps, it was clear she could never have survived.

'Miss Tullow,' insisted Holmes, 'let Doctor Watson take you home. There's nothing more to see here. An officer has just sheeted the body, spare yourself unnecessary grief. Remember Miss Carruthers from happier times, as she was before this terrible business of the stalker came to pass.'

'Oh, Mr Holmes,' she wailed, a trifle unsteady on her feet. I did my best to support her, realising how awful she must feel, her best friend and secretary now lying broken and dead beneath the rotund base of the Norwood clock. 'She meant only for the best and now she joins this Sydney Blackberry. It seems such a tragic waste of two lives.'

'And now, Miss Tullow, we must, I regret to say, consider carefully your own part in the affair.' The efficient Scotland Yarder took out his notebook, gravely licking the lead tip of his pencil before speaking once more. 'How many years had Miss Carruthers been in your employ?'

'Hilda's innocent,' said I, gruffly. 'I believe she was entirely unaware of Miss Carruthers's plan to destroy Sydney Blackberry. She was naturally upset by his continual persecution, but had not the slightest notion a life would be snuffed out because of it.'

'I'll back Watson up on this,' said Holmes, giving me a relentless steely gaze he reserved for miscreants. 'All the evidence we have gathered so far sheds not one jot of blame onto this young lady. Let's not talk ill of Miss Carruthers but shall we just say she was pigheaded, a bit of a bully who gloated on this young man's death. Perhaps she was in love with you, Miss Tullow, by Jove, and saw herself as a medieval knight in shining armour setting off to slay the dragon. Bear with me, Inspector, for I would rather Miss Tullow sleep in her own bed tonight than under lock and key in a police cell. After all, the murderer has gone to face a higher court of justice than ours.'

'You're both of you clear on that point, I trust?' The detective sounded miffed. 'I myself should be inclined to disagree. I put it to you, Miss Tullow, that you were privy to your secretary's murderous intent from the very beginning, an accessory to the crime, if you will.'

'Nonsense,' said I, coming to the lady's defence. 'Hilda – I mean Miss Tullow – taking my professional opinion as a medical man into account, is a cerebral lady of delicate constitution, who has undergone a frightful shock, endured a painful experience because of this stalker's relentless shadowing of her every move. You should pity her, Inspector, not wish to clap her in irons.'

The novelist started to sob uncontrollably. I lent her my handkerchief, placing my arm gently round her slender waist, and guided her away from all the horror of the clock tower, in the strictest propriety, I might add, back to her house in Tennyson Road. Hopkins, I knew, remained sceptical, left to mull over the evidence, but no charges were ever brought against the novelist and, indeed, her books remain as popular today as they were in the winter of 1894.

Whilst writing this narrative, I peruse my modest library and a sentimental tear forms in my eye, for you are correct, dear reader, in the assumption that I was at the time in love with Hilda, although my ardour was naturally never reciprocated. We remained the best of friends until her marriage to the banker Cardosa Felini in 1896, when she quit England altogether to live on the Spanish Riviera, where she has remained ever since. However, that said, our paths were to cross again in the latter part of December.

Mr Sherlock Holmes and myself had been out to visit Bradleys, the tobacconist, when upon our return to our lodgings in Baker Street we were astonished to encounter Miss Hilda Tullow, whom Mrs Hudson had kindly shown in, warming herself by the fire, cosily ensconced in our bachelor apartments. It was, I recall, a bitterly cold morning, with the festival of Christmas just round the corner, our convivial first-floor sitting-room decked out with a few sprigs of holly and ivy upon the mantelpiece. A small decorated Norwegian spruce stood where the old aspidistra plant used to be. However, the reason for her visit was far from festive or cheerful.

'My dear lady,' said Holmes, rushing into his bedroom to remove his scarf and outdoor clothes. 'Thank you for posting us your complimentary copy of your latest book, *The Trials of Lucinda Davenport*. I believe you have it somewhere on your library shelf, Watson?'

'Indeed,' said I, reaching for a cigar from the coal scuttle. 'I have read it from cover to cover in one sitting, so enthralled was I by the plot.' How delighted I was Hilda had decided to call on us and grace us bachelors with her feminine company. 'The weather is foul, is it not? Did you travel on the Metropolitan? They tell me a nasty Arctic rush of air is expected from Siberia towards the end of the week. Snow is sure to follow.'

'You are correct, Mr Holmes, I did travel by subterranean railway. However, I regret to say I have come for your advice regarding –'

'–a decomposing corpse found inside a church porch yesterday. Quite near Tennyson Road, wasn't it?'

'Around the corner from my house, in fact, for it was my own dear little borough church where the body was found.'

'If my memory serves me correctly, young Inspector Hopkins of Scotland Yard, confirmed to me it was the shrouded corpse of the previous incumbent, the Reverend Cranston Howard, buried but five months before at Norwood Hill cemetery.'

'Mr Holmes, shockingly the bones in both arms were apparently snapped, allowing the corpse to adopt a cruciform shape with limbs outstretched.'

'Shockingly? Why, nothing surprises me in a crime of this nature, Miss Tullow. One learns to expect the sordid and more macabre elements.'

'But a church porch, Mr Holmes! A sacred shelter from the rain and wind, where generations of parishioners have gathered for weddings, baptism and funerals – Sunday service!'

'Alas, Miss Tullow, I am entirely unsentimental when it comes to church architecture. One building is very much the same as the next to me – stone, mortar, bricks and rubble. May I smoke?'

195

My companion lit his long cherry wood pipe and began pacing in front of the hearth.

'Be that as it may, I observe you have a singular cloth bag in your hand. You have brought me, I perceive, a solid silver repeater of Swiss make. The same pocket watch left mysteriously amongst the colourfully glazed figurines and manger comprising the traditional nativity scene displayed on trestles further inside the church. It was once the property of the Reverend Howard. Inspector Hopkins filled me in on the details when he visited us earlier. By the way, where is the body stored at present?'

'Why, it is being kept in the church hall, Mr Holmes, the freezing weather of late a considerable aid to preservation.'

'Watson, 'pon my word, we must lose no time. We shall accompany Miss Tullow back to South Norwood; be a good fellow and check the timetable.'

I pulled down our well-thumbed copy of Bradshaw and studied the timetables. 'We've just under half an hour if we want to catch the stopping service, there's also an express to East Croydon which looks promising.'

'Most portentous, my dear fellow. The express will do. East Croydon is not so far from Norwood, is it Miss Tullow?'

'We can take a cab from outside the station directly to Norwood church.'

'Mrs Hudson, Mrs Hudson!' shouted Holmes from the upstairs landing. 'Will you alert young Inspector Stanley Hopkins when he calls later that we are already on our way.'

'Very well, Mr Holmes.'

Upon reaching East Croydon by the express we were eventually conveyed to the church hall in South Norwood by a hired horse and trap. We were greeted at the front of the hall by a doddery old chap with long silver hair and coarse grey whiskers. He wore a frock coat that had seen better days, and peered at us intently over a pair of wire spectacles. I assumed he was the caretaker waiting to let us in, but it turned out he was in fact the medical examiner, a local general practitioner by the name of Doctor Wagstaff.

'I'm just locking up,' said he, sternly. 'The coffee morning's been cancelled.'

'Well, you'd better unlock then because we're here on police business,' said Holmes impatiently.

'Are you Mr Sherlock Holmes?'

'I am the same.'

'An Inspector Hopkins mentioned you would be arriving in South Norwood to help with the case. Good day, Miss Tullow, I didn't recognise you all wrapped up in furs against this bitterly cold weather.'

'He's such a dear old thing,' confided Hilda, taking Holmes's arm as we passed inside. 'He still runs a successful practice along the main road from here, although he is well into his eighties and has a younger partner, Mr Slater, who is away on honeymoon at present and thus unable to attend to the body, else act in the capacity of police surgeon.'

My colleague looked appalled, his wan, hawk-like features betraying every sign of disgust. 'Doctor Wagstaff is in charge of the medical enquiry? Why, I should not trust that fellow to snip my toenails, let alone perform as a pathologist.'

Miss Tullow giggled uncontrollably at my colleague's morose speculation concerning the old fellow's qualifications.

'Mr Holmes,' said she with a smirk, 'you really are quite gay underneath that logical, reasoning, dour exterior.'

'My dear lady, gay or not, there is nothing remotely amusing about a person who would find considerable difficulty doing up his trouser buttons of a morning being put in charge of gathering important forensic evidence.'

Naturally, Hilda declined our invitation to stay a little longer. The faintest whiff of formaldehyde and decomposing organic matter alerted us to a corpse close by. Concealed under a starched white sheet, which I had mistaken for a tea urn and sundry utensils, were the remains of the Reverend Howard, laid out on a trestle table.

With trembling and palsied fingers, the old physician pulled back the sheet.

'What the devil! By Jove, Watson, our Norwood Hill Burke and Hare deserve praise indeed for bringing to light a most singular and controversial issue.'

Half the cadaverous face had been consumed by maggot infestation, but the well-preserved, waxy yellow pallor of the taut skin, the coloration of the lips, the deposits under the nails meant in all likelihood the deceased had been poisoned.

'How many grains of arsenic has this fellow ingested, Watson?'

'A considerable amount,' I replied confidently.

'What's that?' muttered the feeble old doctor,

drooling down the front of his cravat and tie pin, his ears all of a sudden pricking up. 'My own diagnosis should tend towards liver disease brought on by the Reverend Howard's fierce daily imbibing of fine wines and whiskey.'

'A good alternative diagnosis, certainly,' I conceded, my jaded opinion of the old duffer somewhat diminished. 'However, I should still plump for arsenic.'

'But that would indicate foul play, gentlemen,' said he, frowning.

'Precisely,' remarked my colleague, preparing to leave, giving the specimen's genitalia a final inquisitive prod with his cane. 'Bravo, that is all we shall require on the pathology front for now. Good day, doctor, we are off in search of lunch.'

We discovered a decent restaurant along the High Street and during our meal I was fascinated to learn what Holmes had deduced from the deceased vicar's silver repeater.

'Observe, my dear Watson, the hands are stopped at six o'clock precisely. Quite possibly to subtly convey something of crucial importance regarding the vicar's untimely end.'

'Was there anything concealed inside?' I asked, sipping my tea, leaning over as Holmes, using his trusty pipe knife, prised open the watch cover. He smiled appreciatively, retrieving a small piece of tissue paper neatly folded into four, upon which was written in red ink the number one.

'By Jove, Watson, this really is a lark. Dobson shall

find this case a real stickler, but for myself I begin to understand.'

'What absurdity,' I chuckled. 'Holmes, I have not the faintest clue what the hands of a pocket watch positioned at six o'clock represent, nor the number one in red ink, but I know you're on to something, old chap.'

'Oh, you know I am – I am,' he answered, taking out his pipe and striking a Vesta to light it. 'Now, follow my simple reasoning – at six o'clock.'

'Understood.'

'Four folds of the tissue paper plus numero one written in red ink equals–'

'Fourteen, yes I'm with you.'

'A connection to the church, the porch even.'

'At six o'clock, fourteen persons.'

'Naturally. Now consider the shrouded corpse, forcibly manipulated into a cruciform shape.'

'A cross, a brass crucifix.'

'Prominently displayed whereabouts in our church?'

'The altar.'

'Bravo, Watson, you nearly have it.'

'The stalls, the church choir meets at six o'clock.'

'You excel yourself, dear boy. Red ink incidentally represents the coloured cloth of ecclesiastical cassocks. Ah, Inspector Hopkins, you look frozen. The freezing cloud of Arctic air from Siberia lurks ever closer. You are welcome to share our little feast. Might I recommend the vegetarian? Or the chicken omelette? There's plenty of fresh tea in the pot. Help yourself to a cup and saucer.'

The detective nodded. 'Well, it's a dire business

Mr Holmes. I've just been over to the church hall to view the body. Why couldn't they have left the poor clergyman to rest in peace? At this time of year, too. It's quite turned my stomach. Dobson, the local man, is fagged out asking questions and getting nowhere. I believe he's up at Norwood Hill cemetery ferreting around. I will have a portion of that delicious omelette if I may.'

'So what does Scotland Yard's most ambitious officer make of it all, the shrouded corpse in the porch, and so forth?'

'A ritual of some kind maybe, Mr Holmes.' The detective poured some tea and mulled the thing through. 'I'd hate to mention Satanists, but there's no telling what these practitioners of the black arts get up to. Snapping the bones of his arms – dreadful.'

'Be that as it may, contrary to your dark hypothesis, a point is trying to be made here. Someone wishes to tell us something of importance in a positive way, but using a macabre code.'

'From beyond the grave, you mean. You're not insisting we bring in a medium? I'll not stand for that.'

Holmes smoked his pipe, creating a pall of wafting tobacco smoke which clung to the restaurant ceiling.

'Satanists aside, have you considered someone may have poisoned the vicar, before he was laid beneath the ground, I mean?'

'Poisoned? Now that really is quite fantastical. Old Doctor Wagstaff, whom the local constabulary have appointed to look into the matter, is a most senior and knowledgeable medical practitioner who informed me that the Reverend Howard died from

201

liver failure brought on by a lifetime of heavy drinking. He was overly fond of wine and whiskey apparently.'

'The symptoms of arsenic poisoning closely resemble alcohol-related diseases, but Holmes and myself have over the years seen enough of these cases to make a sound judgment, as have you, Inspector Hopkins,' said I, lighting a cigarette and settling back in my chair after my meal.

'Blowed if I haven't, Doctor Watson. All right, I'd agree the skin coloration and condition of certain of the body organs points towards your arsenic theory, but it's hardly conclusive. Anyhow, Mr Holmes, supposing you're correct and it was murder? How do we go about solving the case?'

'Firstly,' said my colleague, puffing reflectively on his pipe while gazing out of the restaurant window at the slow-moving carriage traffic clattering past, 'I think we can pay a visit to Tennyson Road. It is time for the popular author Miss Tullow to play her part. I should like to question her about the congregation who attend the local parish church of a Sunday, the members of the choir in particular.'

Braving the chilly winter weather we walked briskly along Selhurst Road past the borough church. Norwood clock tower, the scene of the mayhem surrounding Miss Carruthers's death, caused little comment. It seemed to me Holmes was entirely focused on the case at hand, striding purposefully along the tree-lined pavement to number 27.

How pleasant it was to be once more ensconced

but a week before Christmas in Hilda's cheery red brick villa in Tennyson Road. This time we sat in the drawing-room, relaxed and smoking our pipes. The dear lady seemed quite reconciled to her ordeal concerning the stalker Sydney Blackberry, being talkative and wonderful company, wholly at ease with her homely, festive surroundings, for there was a glittering Christmas fir tree adorned with colourful baubles and strands of tinsel in one corner and the mantelpiece was bedecked with holly and ivy, paper bells and chains and other ornamental decorations.

'May I start by asking you, Miss Tullow, if your late secretary Miss Carruthers was ever a member of the church choir?'

'Indeed, Mr Holmes, Kate often sang at both morning service and evensong of a Sunday.'

'Did she possess a pleasant voice?'

'A passable baritone. Our venerable old organist nurtured her voice, if you will, taking time at choir practice to teach her to sing more from the diaphragm. She enjoyed being a member of the church choir very much.'

'When does the choir practice take place?'

'Every Tuesday at six o'clock in the evening, Mr Holmes. Did any one of you attend Sydney Blackberry's funeral in Croydon?' asked Hilda.

'I did.' Inspector Stanley Hopkins' face broadened in a grin. 'Us policemen are always interested as to who turns up at a criminal's funeral, ma'am. And there's always the sherry and cake afterwards, of course.' He chuckled, completely misjudging the general mood.

'Miss Carruthers's body was, I hear, returned to

her family in Hertfordshire for burial,' said I, 'the coffin travelling down by train. Do you miss her, Hilda?'

'Terribly,' she confessed. 'Oh Doctor Watson, although she was a bit of a gruff, snarling bulldog on occasions she looked after my affairs wonderfully. However, the new girl, Miss Chalmers, from an agency in town, is competent and gets on with the job, so I've no complaints. What have you discovered about the body in the porch mystery, Mr Holmes? I must confess to you, I once encountered the Reverend Howard stumbling out of church reeking of drink. He was incapable of stringing a sentence together and could barely stand up straight. A member of my congregation told me that on one occasion he was actually inebriated whilst delivering a sermon and she walked out. He was far from popular in South Norwood, I can tell you.'

'The issue of alcohol has already surfaced, my dear. To all intents and purposes old Doctor Wagstaff is convinced that Howard died of natural causes from chronic liver failure. I and Doctor Watson, on the other hand, believe him to have been poisoned by a large quantity of arsenic.'

'Murdered! Oh, how beastly,' Hilda exclaimed. 'But why, Mr Holmes? I admit he was a taciturn, rude individual, a man of the cloth who rarely appeared to care for his flock, but – murder. Now that really is going too far. I personally should favour Doctor Wagstaff's prognosis. The clergyman drank like a fish, Mr Holmes. I believe he was an alcoholic.'

'We, Miss Tullow, believe he was poisoned,' said Holmes flatly, a trifle irritated by Hilda's firm stance.

'By a member of your church choir.' He had dropped the bombshell.

'Are you inferring Miss Carruthers had something to do with this?'

'At this juncture, no one can be discounted, madam. But yes, I am.'

That same evening we took a slow train to Victoria. It was fearfully bitter, with temperatures dipping well below zero. By the time we returned to Baker Street. I felt sure the morning would be sharp and cold, leaving our window panes encrusted and edged with filigree frost work.

We were glad to be once more basking in the familiar surroundings of our sitting-room, a cheery fire ablaze in the grate, and yet, truth be told, Holmes could not settle. He could not be still. He paced up and down our sitting-room absently, adjusting the gas pressure of the globe lamp, picking up a newspaper, thereafter flinging it aside, until at last his lean, lithe figure slumped in his favourite armchair and with long, bony fingers steepled beneath his chin, my colleague at last began to expound on the Norwood case.

'For some time now,' said he, taking his pipe and refilling it from the Persian slipper with the strongest shag tobacco, 'the problem of the wedding dress has been perplexing me, an issue that refuses to go away. Watson, are you listening?'

'What? Oh yes, please continue, Holmes,' said I dreamily, for in truth I was miles away, my mind dwelling on the beautiful Hilda, small of stature yet a formidably sharp and intelligent woman who could effortlessly ensnare a man's heart.

'I have, since Miss Carruthers's death, been of the sound opinion that the bridal gown has a deeper significance. Watson, you're not paying attention!'

'Eh, sorry, old chap. What did you say? Something about the wedding dress?' My voice betrayed a nonchalant awareness of the facts concerning the case, a 'couldn't care less' attitude which I knew my friend could easily detect.

'Are you perchance thinking about your old regiment, the war?'

'What, Afghanistan? No, I am glad to be out of it. My days as a daring young army surgeon are long gone.'

'You are in love then.'

'Holmes, what confounded –'

'Admit it, Watson. Oh I saw you were a bit fresh with her back at Norwood clock tower. The author Hilda Tullow is the object of your misguided affections and you just can't stop thinking about her. You have observed she wears neither a wedding nor engagement ring. She is not in your mind betrothed, a foolish inference, for modern women dispense with such trinkets of loyalty and long-term partnership.'

'That's heartless and crass,' said I, incensed.

'If you had taken the trouble to study your Greek, you should have avoided this lovesick condition. I recall how Ulysses and his men came to be dashed to pieces on the rocks because of a siren's call.'

'You're right,' said I, accepting my drubbing. 'I am in love with Hilda, but in future I must learn to keep my emotions in check. Pray continue with your observations upon the Norwood case, Holmes.'

'We are still not clear why Miss Carruthers took so much care to dress up the corpse of Sydney Blackberry in a bridal gown. At first, I imagined Hilda Tullow's book, *The Scarecrow Bride*, was the inspiration, but now I'm not so sure.'

'The story concerns a humble mill girl murdered on the eve of her wedding to Captain Carson. Consequently a mysterious scarecrow draped in a bridal gown is placed on her grave at Dunstead churchyard.'

'But it bears little resemblance to our real-life crime where a determined stalker was murdered.'

'I suppose not.'

'My dear Watson, there is only really one course. I propose we interview every single member of that church choir, including the organist. We cannot ignore the fact that the Reverend Howard could have been poisoned to death.'

The following morning, we returned to South Norwood in good spirits. A light fall of snow during the night had settled, but was quickly melting as the sun came up. The High Street's festive decorations were delightful to behold and yet strangely incongruous when one considered, as Christmas approached, the body of a murdered clergyman had yet to be removed from the church hall, a serious crime dominating the local press, South Norwood taking on an infamous if unfair reputation of being something more akin to a 'murder capital' than a respectable suburb of Croydon.

We bumped into the vicar of the parish, Cedric Small, a popular and well-liked figure in the community.

'Good morning, vicar. How are you today?'

'Fine, thank you. A pity about this wretched decomposing corpse, though. I have admonished Dobson, our local man, in the strongest terms, insisting the body be removed by Friday before we have our annual Christmas Fayre. Doreen Carter told me only yesterday she requires the trestle table for urns, jugs, cups and saucers, teapots and cutlery. The tea ladies are quite understandably upset.'

'I'm sure it shall be a great success,' remarked Holmes, anxious to move on, for the vicar's small talk rankled with him.

'Good day to you both,' said he, cordially raising his hat.

'Good day to you, vicar,' we replied.

We were passing the boot and shoemaker's shop along Norwood High Street when the undertaker atop of a passing glass-panelled hearse, threw something at us. Before we could respond, a weighty, sealed package landed in a nearby pile of slush beside the kerb and we watched as the coal-black horses galloped off and the ostrich-plumed funeral carriage hurtled up the road, lost to the general traffic.

My colleague leant down, seizing the damp package before ripping off the sodden brown paper, anxious to discover what was wrapped inside.

'What the deuce is this? By Jove, Watson, it's an

empty chemist's bottle of arsenic. See the warning skull and crossbones displayed prominently upon the label and, believe it or not, there's a message inside if only we could get at it.'

It took an age to manipulate the thin roll of tissue paper out of the neck of the chemist's bottle, but perseverance eventually won through. The note was written in prescription Latin, so I perceived, and I guessed at once who it was from.

'Well, dear fellow, would you be good enough to confirm my approximate translation? "Meet me at my surgery along Selhurst Road – Wagstaff".'

'I concur.'

The doctor's three-storey house formed part of an eastern terrace featuring a cream stucco exterior with a Doric pillar entrance for his surgery and waiting room. There was a handsome balustrade balcony above the first-floor sashed window.

'Come in, gentlemen, come in. Good morning, Mr Holmes, and you too, Doctor Watson. The days grow colder, do they not? The great Siberian pall shall soon be upon us. A white Christmas in prospect. By all means, smoke. I shall join you in a celebration of Madame Niccotina's fine, soothing qualities by relighting my own pipe. Please take your seats by the fire.'

We had been shown by a manservant into the medical practitioner's oak-panelled study and music room, a gloomy, curtained sanctum lit by a single lamp upon the pedal organ. Sheet music abounded, the floor to ceiling shelves stocked with musical scores and rows of vellum-bound titles, amongst them a complete set of Poe and Robert Louis Stevenson.

After he had struck a match to his meerschaum, barely managing to keep the Vesta steady for his palsied hands trembled so much, he parted his long, silvery hair and gazed at each of us in turn for a long while before saying finally: 'I am the organist, I am the choirmaster and, gentlemen, I am the mastermind responsible for the slaying of young Sydney Blackberry and the loathsome clergyman Howard.'

'You were responsible for digging him up and displaying his shrouded remains in the porch?'

'It was a little whim of mine I could not resist. I wished above all to set clues for you, to test your abilities, Mr Holmes – I have long been a devotee of the capital's famous consulting detective and have followed your cases avidly, penned so admirably, if I may say so, by your acclaimed biographer Doctor Watson. We ourselves are untouchable, there is no evidence that can possibly bring us to trial.'

'I realise that,' said Holmes. 'You and who else were responsible for their deaths?'

'All of us, the entire choir, boys, men and ladies are linked stronger than any society of freemasons. To wait for that drunkard the Reverend Howard's incumbency to naturally run its course should have been intolerable. Once Mr Layton, the church warden, discovered the unmentionable truth of this man, his life was effectively ended. All of us were agreed it would be better for both of them to die.'

'The unmentionable truth?' said I. 'What unmentionable truth?'

'That the Reverend Cranston Howard and Sydney Blackberry were lovers. They were having an affair.

Stalking Miss Tullow was a vile enough crime, but this...'

'And you mentioned earlier you planned their deaths,' said I.

'Miss Carruthers being wholly responsible for the dirty work, of course. Upon my strict instructions she agreed to befriend the clergyman and would often pop over to the vicarage and make him a brew. He came to trust her, I think, which was a tremendous mistake, very unwise, for the levels of arsenic were gradually increased in his tea. By the end he was insensible and fell into a poisoned stupor from which he never recovered.'

'And then you dealt with the young man from Croydon.'

'The blushing bride. Oh yes, we dealt most effectively with that horrid specimen of humanity. The upsetting nature of his shadowing of Miss Tullow, a dear, sweet friend, particularly galled. The sharpened knitting needle as a murder weapon I am most proud of devising. It will never be traced, of course. We covered our tracks well.'

'You regard yourself as a masterly adversary. I congratulate you, Doctor Wagstaff.'

'I take that as the greatest compliment of my long life, Mr Holmes. The little clues of late were, I trust, appreciated.'

'Sublimely so.'

Coming out of the doctor's surgery back into the sleet, we were confronted by Dobson, the local man. The Inspector looked very out of sorts.

'Well I'm blowed, gentlemen. I've been on this case for the best part of a week and I'm still no nearer to making an arrest, nor understanding why in heaven's name a bloomin' decomposing corpse should end up dumped on my patch. An' now I've got Cedric Small the vicar on my back just 'cos I commandeered his church hall.'

He walked off in a huff, crossing the main road, pausing to take out his wallet before entering the nearby tobacconist.

'What's to be done about Doctor Wagstaff?' said I, unfurling my umbrella. 'From what I could gather he seems to think murder is a bit like a game of happy families.'

'And I wonder which card he plans to deal next, Watson. His vigilante antics cannot go unpunished. The law in England is clear on that. But he's right, it would be the devil's own job to bring him to stand trial. Him and that church choir of his are on a par with the Sicilian Mafia, the late, lamented Miss Carruthers being the nominated so-called 'hit man', as our American cousins would say. Halloa, well I'm darned!' Holmes remarked with a note of fondness in his voice. 'Isn't that young Stanley Hopkins coming up the road from the station?'

The Scotland Yard detective waved from across the road upon recognising his friends.

'Ah, Hopkins,' said Holmes, shaking his hand in greeting. 'How's our tenacious Scotland Yarder this morning?'

'Pretty grim, Mr Holmes, pretty grim. I'm in need of a half decent lead, for this matter of the body in the porch has got me flummoxed. I have just an inkling the body we found in the train and this decomposing clergyman may be linked in some way, but how, I've no idea.'

'We have made considerable inroads, Inspector,' interjected my companion. 'However, you would be hard pressed to make an arrest, let alone discover enough evidence to hang the master criminal involved.'

'Master criminal? My, my, Mr Holmes, is Professor Moriarty in on this caper then, for if so you are correct. The Yard's got nothing on him, he always remains in the background, allowing others to take the rap!'

'I should say this man is in certain respects far more ruthless and clever than the professor,' said I with feeling, puffing on a cigarette.

'More ruthless, cleverer, you say? Now that is praise indeed, Doctor Watson.'

If anything, it had grown colder and the sheeting sleet had now been transformed into a howling blizzard. We hurried across the road, congested with horse-drawn vehicles of every description, to take shelter in a convenient shop doorway.

We had not stood there long, stamping our feet and brushing the snow off our overcoats and hats, despondently gazing into the 'whiteout'. Visibility was down to a few yards and omnibus and carriage traffic along South Norwood High Street crawled to a virtual standstill, when surprisingly a wailing yeti, as it appeared to us, came stumbling out of the driving snow. 'He's been shot, he's been shot!' cried a muffled voice.

'Miss Tullow!' Holmes shouted, for he somehow

recognised the novelist, recalling the immense fur coat she always wore. 'In here quickly.'

'He's been shot, Mr Holmes.'

'Calm yourself, madam. Who's been shot?'

'The vicar, Cedric Small,' she gasped, pulling herself together. 'I've just been round to the vicarage where I was to go over final preparations for the children's Christmas nativity play, which I am organising this year. Barely had I been shown into the hall by Mary, the housekeeper, when we heard three shots ring out. Thereafter we discovered Cedric on the floor of his study, lying in a pool of blood. He's alive, but weakening. You must come at once, Doctor Watson, Mary's hysterical.'

Without another word our party of pedestrians set off along the main road, determined to brave the wintry conditions. By the time we reached the vicarage the blizzard had petered out, the wind dropped and it was snowing only in blowy flakes.

I took Hilda's arm and we entered the house, where a distraught Mary, in tears and on the precipice of a complete breakdown, led us to the vicar's study. I could see right away the Reverend Small had a shoulder wound that was bleeding profusely.

'You'll live,' said I, forcing a brandy flask to his dry lips while Miss Tullow went in search of a bowl of warm water, a bottle of iodine and plentiful bandages.

'It was that blackguard Dobson,' he gasped. 'A policeman in the pay of "The Choirmaster". There is a league of them, all in this together, Mr Holmes.'

'Steady Small, here, take a sip of brandy,' said he, leaning over to support the clergyman's head.

'That much we have already gathered. Doctor Wagstaff crowed of his many murderous accomplishments at the surgery earlier where I and Doctor Watson were invited to be his captive audience for a summary of his "vigilante" career so far. I suspected something infamous was afoot, but when and where eluded me. So you are on to him I take it.'

The vicar swallowed and weakly nodded. 'While changing my surplice the other morning in the vestry I overheard two members of the choir, Smith and Trent, whispering in low voices about the ease with which they had dug up Howard's corpse and transported it from Norwood Hill cemetery to the church porch, always referring in hushed, secretive tones to "The Choirmaster", like he was their leader.'

'Which of course he is.'

'Well, Mr Holmes, "The Choirmaster" is Doctor Wagstaff.'

'Precisely.'

'I additionally heard mention of "the liberal usage of arsenic" when listening in to their conversation.'

'And you rightly deduced that the Reverend Howard's murder was sanctioned by the choir as a whole.'

'Exactly. I was about to confront the doctor personally. I had written him a note addressing my concerns.'

'Unwise. Despite his doddery, palsied appearance, he is a clever thinker and must have realised his invisibility was at risk and that you suspected something. To summarise, we are all of us in considerable danger. Are you fit?'

'Much better, thank you, Mr Holmes.'

'Merely a flesh wound,' said I. 'Luckily, Dobson is a poor shot. His aim was all over the place because his hands were shaking so much, I surmise.'

'His incompetence is legendary,' said Stanley Hopkins, peering at a couple of stray bullet marks on the far wall, displacing the plaster. 'Lucky for you, Small, it was not the late Miss Carruthers sanctioned to carry out the assassination or you should have been dead by now.'

There was a timid knock at the vicarage door. Nobody took much notice, save for Mary the housekeeper, who rushed out into the hall. I confess I was more concerned for Small's recovery, glad he was now able to stand up unaided, his right arm confined to a sling improvised by myself and Hilda from an old shirt of his. I was wondering what more I could do for my 'patient on the mend' when of all people, who should step into the vicar's study, the scene of the bungled assassination attempt, but Mr Croft, the supervisor from the Selhurst depot, dressed in his grey work overalls and oily flat cap.

'Inspector Hopkins, I was told you were here at the vicarage by a bobby on the beat. I have important news. I came straight from the depot. The entire yard is in uproar, the railwaymen wringing their hands in despair.'

'Why's that, Mr Croft?' the detective said warily. 'No more naked bodies on trains if you please. The last one warranted a considerable amount of police time and effort.'

'Nothing like that, it's worse. A train has been stolen. A Terrier Class locomotive and a single passenger coach normally kept on a siding for usage as a special. Here, let's 'ave that flask of brandy. I'm in need of a stiff drink.'

'A train stolen, you say.'

'Yes, I told you sir, a special. Signalmen all along the route of the southern main line have been alerted and ordered to give the "line clear". The Croydon Suburban shall never hear the last of it.'

'It all makes perfect sense,' said Small, a perplexed expression darkening his youthful features.

'What does?' asked my companion.

'Mr Smith, the basso and Mr Trent, the counter tenor, a singer of some merit, are both members of the church choir, and at the same time work on the railway. Mr Smith is a train driver, Trent a professional fireman. They're train crew of many years experience, on expresses also.'

'So, Doctor Wagstaff wasted little time commandeering the services of these footplate sycophants, but to what end?' wondered Holmes.

'To escape,' Stanley Hopkins piped up. 'To escape because he has got it into that clever head of his that we are soon to arrest him and ransack his vigilante organisation "The Choir".'

'Bravo, Hopkins.'

'Good gracious, but where to Holmes?' said I.

'Victoria, my dear Watson. It is the boat train to the Continent that is so precious to him. If I remember my Bradshaw correctly, there is only one service a day upon the week leading to Christmas, and by Jove, that is cutting it fine.'

'Aye sir, no doubt he'll shunt up on a siding at a lesser station like Clapham and make a run for it from there in a cab. Mr Hopkins, you'd better telegraph ahead. Terrier Class, fired-up boiler – Lor' they must have got into the depot afore dawn. This Smith fella knows his locomotives all right.'

Inspector Hopkins put on his hat and overcoat and, along with Mr Croft, went off in search of the nearest post office in South Norwood.

While Mary, herself feeling much revived after her frightening experience, banked up the coal fire and settled the invalid into his favourite armchair, spoiling the vicar with a bowl of rich chicken broth, Miss Tullow, myself and Holmes bid the Reverend Small good morning and passed out of the front door directly onto the snow-covered lawn, the fresh, biting air of a freezing winter's day reviving our zest for life, our thoughts tending to turn towards the Christmas holidays.

'Do you like a turkey for Christmas lunch, Doctor Watson?' asked Hilda, wrapped up in her enormous fur coat to fend off the cold, squeezing my arm.

'We generally have goose,' said I, as we strolled towards the wrought iron gate. Sherlock Holmes reaching it first, held it open to allow us through. We gathered to say our farewells on the icy pavement.

'Well, goodbye, Mr Holmes, and you too Doctor Watson. I trust the trains are not running late at Norwood Junction and let's hope and pray they manage to detain Doctor Wagstaff and his accomplices at the boat train terminus. I should like to see Dobson hang for his murderous attempt on the vicar's life.'

* * *

Hilda and I were embracing. We had just waltzed round the glittering ballroom, effortlessly gliding in each other's joy, lost for words, breathless as only two sweethearts can be.

'You are the most handsome man in England, John.'

'And you,' said I, 'the prettiest woman. You are the girl of my dreams, Hilda, I can't live without you. I loved you from the first time I ever saw you.'

'Wasn't that at Tennyson Road?'

'Yes, I recall your profile. You were preening yourself in front of the mirror.

'John.'

'Darling.'

'Might I have this next dance? They're playing Lumbye's "Champagne Galop".'

She hesitated at first, then leaned gently forward. I could not help it, I seized her passionately in my arms, not giving a damn for etiquette. Our noses brushed, our lips almost . . .

'Watson, Watson, wake up man, there's urgent news, this is no time to be taking a nap on the sofa. Mrs Hudson's supper was interrupted by a constable of police from the transport section. She's livid.'

'Good heavens,' I yawned. 'It's late afternoon already, Holmes. The curtains are drawn. What's up?'

My colleague bounded across the room in a haze of pipe smoke. He rummaged on his desk then returned bearing a slip of paper. We had both of us only got back to our lodgings but an hour or so previous, and I was whacked.

'I'll read the message, Watson. "This afternoon a special collided with a passenger service just outside Clapham Junction. The derailed coaches smashed into the back of each other. Many were old rolling stock lit by compressed oil gas, and a fire has broken out. Points failure or fatal lapse of memory on behalf of the signalman may have been the cause. At this stage there are twelve fire pumps in attendance at the scene." The note is from Stanley Hopkins.'

So it was that Doctor Wagstaff's luck finally ran out, his daring scheme in ruins. The next morning every newspaper was full of the details concerning "The Clapham Smash", as the popular press called it, but it is from a trusted broadsheet, the *Daily Telegraph* for Friday December 19th 1894, that I shall let the discerning reader digest the full horror of what happened.

The train smash in which twenty-two people died was apparently caused by signalman Bunce, who failed to remember that a special was due and forgot to follow through the correct signal procedure, thus at Clapham Junction the signal arm should have shown the 'DANGER' position but, instead, indicated 'LINE CLEAR'.

The first Bunce knew of the disaster, prior to the special and passenger service being wrecked, was when he received a telegraph bell signal indicating 'BE READY FOR EXPRESS SPECIAL', but by this time, despite a last ditch effort to stop the train by means of a red lamp, a collision was unavoidable. Needless to say the night of clearance was a long and ghastly one.

A fortnight following Christmas, the breakfast things cleared away, a sunny, frosty morning in progress, Holmes and myself were seated either side of a roaring fire partaking of our second cup of coffee, studying the broadsheets, when Mrs Hudson flitted in and placed a plain brown manila envelope on the arm of my companion's chair. He languidly reached for the paper knife, slit open the envelope and read the contents, a grim and calculating expression emerging on his pale, hawk-like features. Scraping out the bowl of my briar pipe, I instinctively felt a sense of unease.

'Who's it from, Holmes?'

He tossed the letter across for me to glance over. I could make little of it.

'Another of your riddles,' I yawned. 'How many of these unsigned and unsolicited letters do we receive every year? Hundreds, I should imagine, from complete strangers. You know where it belongs, old man, in the wastepaper basket.'

'I should stay my hand regarding this singular conundrum, my dear fellow, for it contains a perplexing message.'

'Message? What possible communication can you deduce from this verbage?'

'A clever antagonist is the sender, I fear, one known to us from the recent past.'

'Moriarty? Surely not,' said I in earnest, cleaning out and knocking my pipe against the brass fender.

'Not he. I shall elaborate. Cast your eye over the wording once more. The right-hand side, reading down the page.'

I sighed and did as Holmes had requested. 'The message reads thus,' said I.

Mr Holmes,
I must discipline,
coach you,
sir.
Viva La France.
Are you willing?

'I'm none the wiser, the ramblings of a lunatic.'

'On the contrary, all the clues are there, perfectly placed. One only needs to apply the requisite skills to decipher the code, thus the message is plain and simple to understand.' He paused to relight his pipe.

'I must discipline – a puppy dog for instance.'

'Train it?' said I.

'Train – the first word, now one down.'

'Coach.'

'Next.'

'Sir.'

'Amend to sur.'

'Viva.'

'Survive.'

'And the final word "are" is quite simply changed to the letter "r", thus the completed message reads "train coach survivor".'

'Good gracious, you don't mean to tell me Doctor Wagstaff is alive?'

'I'm afraid that is the case. Halloa, what's this shouting on the stairs? We have a distressed female visitor, Watson. This shall require all your reserves of charm and expertise – the fairer sex is your department, I believe.'

'Mr Holmes, Mr Holmes, it cannot be, it cannot be, but it's true,' said the lady bursting into our front sitting-room, pursued by our esteemed and tenacious Scottish housekeeper. 'South Norwood must endure one of its most tragic losses of recent times. So young, a whole life in front of him snuffed out.'

'Calm yourself, Miss Tullow. There, my dear, take the sofa, let me take your things. Mrs Hudson, a pot of strong India tea, if you will. Watson, shift yourself from that comfy armchair and prepare a sedative for the young lady.'

'A house fire over at the vicarage. Cedric Small was burned to death in his own bed. He stood no chance. Mary tried to intervene but the intensity of the flames kept her back. The top storey of the vicarage has gone up in smoke. Nothing remains but a burnt-out shell. The local Norwood engine is at the scene, as are four steam fire pumps from Croydon brigade.'

'Cedric Small, you say, the poor clergyman wounded in the shooting incident just prior to Christmas. I don't like this one bit, Watson. Have you that tincture of opium handy? Here, madam, sip this, it shall stimulate calmness.'

'What must you think of me, gentlemen?' she gasped, drinking from the tiny cup, 'coming up to London like this, but when I saw from my bedroom window sparks and smoke rising into the sky, flames above the roof tops and chimney pots, I knew it must be the vicarage. I learnt of the poor clergyman's death from a fire brigade captain at the scene.'

'It's always so unfair when an avoidable accident occurs,' said I. 'A house fire rages in seconds, the roof timbers and lagging catch alight. Thereby the attic and upper story bear the brunt.'

'Avoidable accident? I doubt that very much,' my companion sneered.

'The blaze was started deliberately then?'

'I think so.'

'Dobson?'

'Else one of the others of the gang. Miss Tullow, I must draw your attention to an unfortunate letter I received this morning, a coded message, as a matter of fact. From what I have deduced so far, I have to tell you Doctor Wagstaff survived the Clapham smash.'

'Alive – oh my Lord, that monster still in our midst. He exists.'

'Indeed, the fire may well have been the result of his fiendish grip on the vigilante group "The Choir"! However, who was the actual perpetrator responsible for setting the vicarage alight we may never know. While Doctor Wagstaff lives, danger lurks at every turn. Watson, have you Bradshaw's handy? We must return to South Norwood with the minimum of delay. There is an express from London Bridge to Norwood Junction. My dear Miss Tullow, are you up to travelling?'

'I believe so. The shock of all that has quite unsettled me.'

'Hilda, finish your sedative,' said I, 'it will calm your nerves no end.'

'I believe I am quite recovered, thank you, Doctor Watson,' she said, passing me the beaker.

By the time we reached Norwood, the ruined vicarage was still smouldering. Firemen were up on ladders hacking at the charred debris of collapsed roof timbers, the odd small fire here and there still flickering before becoming extinguished by a dousing of water from a bucket.

'It's a bad business,' said my colleague as we stood upon the frosty pavement considering the wreckage of a home, listening to the thumping of axes and hissing of rising steam, a burnt-out old bed still visible upon the top storey, the wire coiled springs charred and blackened, the mattress, and presumably the poor vicar being wholly immolated by the force and intensity of the heat.

Whilst we casually stood about with the crowd of onlookers who had by now begun dispersing, Hilda, dressed in her voluminous fur coat at my side, clinging to my arm, an unusual and bizarre occurrence took place, for an ostrich-plumed glass-panelled hearse led by a group of coal-black mares drew up beside us, the snorting, well-groomed horses trotting to a standstill.

No one took much heed for the very smell of death permeated the frozen air.

A short individual, one of the frock-coated, top-hatted undertakers, got down and calmly held a pistol, persisting in digging it into Miss Tullow's ribs.

'No tricks, step into the rear of the hearse, if you please. All of you, the doctor's carriage awaits. The coffin bier, wooden rollers and nickel rail have been removed, plush leather seating installed, an interior design of his own personal invention of which he is naturally very proud. You will find every

225

convenience provided, fine cigars, a decanter of "Old Ruby". Eh, one moment, Doctor Watson, allow my companion to frisk you if you don't mind. We don't want frightful mistakes involving a loaded firearm to occur en route to the depot.'

'Selhurst depot,' said I incredulously, supporting Miss Tullow as her dainty little frame stepped up into the rear of the parked hearse.

'Correct sir, an exclusively private siding where Doctor Wagstaff's special carriage awaits shunting, to commence thereafter a speedy and uncomplicated journey to his ancestral home in Surrey. Croydon, then Purley, Tadworth, Tattenham Corner and Caterham shall be our route. My name's Trent by the way, and this is Mr Albert Smith. Train crew for the day.'

'You were driving and coaling the Terrier engine. How the devil did you both escape the train smash at Clapham Junction? You were surely on the footplate.'

'Hush, all shall be revealed soon enough. A fine bottle of Moët and Chandon pink champagne is being kept on ice to commemorate this splendid reunion.'

The rear carriage doors were shut and locked tight, leaving us to marvel at the sheer splendour of the interior. Even a light snack of cold cutlets, cheese and ham, and a leaf salad had been provided, set out on a sprung collapsible table along with crystal glasses and silverware. Needless to relate, the memory of the Reverend Howard's deteriorating, arsenic-absorbed corpse laid out in the village hall curbed our appetites somewhat.

No sooner had the funeral carriage trotted off down the road, than my esteemed colleague Mr Sherlock Holmes began to fret, for he strongly suspected, because of the enclosed airtight environment, that we should become the unwitting victims of sulphur gas pumped through a concealed vent, but this turned out not to be the case and we arrived at the Selhurst depot without incident.

The glass-sided hearse was parked up on an entry road of the goods yard alongside a single box van – box van! I thought, that's a bit of a come-down. Where was this private carriage that was talked of? It was a plain and functional goods wagon with whitewashed letters painted on the side: CROYDON SUBURBAN RAILWAY COMPANY.

We were let out and left to it for the horse-drawn, ostrich-plumed hearse set off at a gallop and we never saw it again.

Holmes was first to clamber into the goods van whilst I did my best to assist Hilda up the gantry steps, careful to prevent any greasy oil from the rusty coupling marking her skirts.

'He's been laid out, Watson,' my colleague shouted from within the gloomy interior. 'Left for the hungry dogs and vultures, by the look of it.'

Inside I perceived a rough wooden packing crate lined with dingy straw was left open, its lid unnailed, the body of our one-time adversary reclining of course, sleeping the sleep of the just, the elderly medical practitioner at rest at last, a satisfied smile on his lips.

'He's been dead only a few hours,' said I. 'Rigor mortis has set in, notice the flatulent smell.'

'And see, here's an envelope clasped between cold, dead fingers, addressed to me. Prise it out, there's a good fellow. Miss Tullow, might I recommend the corner bench further down? We are going to be a while, I fear. That's it, sit down and make yourself at home.'

I managed to retrieve the envelope and immediately passed it to my colleague, who tore it open.

For the discerning reader, I have reproduced the doctor's letter here in its entirety and thus end this narrative on a note of positive optimism, for South Norwood is free at last from this evil man and his clever, murderous schemes.

My dear Holmes,

Alas, by the time you read this epistle, 'St Vitus's Dance', of which I have been a long-term, terminal sufferer, shall have claimed my life and I should not be able to address you personally. We deliberately smashed the hurtling engine into the carriages of the slow moving passenger train just outside Clapham to divert unwanted attention, and the machinations of Scotland Yard, who it seemed were closing in on my well-perfected plan to escape the country. It was a piffling matter of securing a lever onto maximum steam pressure here, else loosening a brake pipe there, the mechanical expertise not my own, you understand, rather members of 'The Choir', Mr Trent and Mr Smith, (both of whom will have escaped justice wonderfully by the time you read this).

Jumping from the moving train proved irksome, yet rewarding. A suitably banked curve meant the engine crawled along at slow speed before the locomotive was put into maximum acceleration, just before Clapham. My escape route was thus secure. Alas, before I could reach the boat train terminus at Victoria the following day, after lying low in a guest house in Herne Hill, my already aged and diminished constitution drastically took a turn for the worse and the tremors and shaking in my limbs increased to the point it was felt desirable to return to my home in Norwood, and it was here in my study under the increasing usage of opiates I decided upon a final statement of my intent by disposing of that troublesome young man, the vicar Cedric Small – all Dobson's work incidentally.

What a thrill watching from the comfort of my front room as the house burnt down. How the blood coursed through my brittle veins. The St Vitus appeared to retreat, but only for a short while because it returned with a vengeance this morning. I am a chronic invalid. Having had long practice at the bedside of others sick and infirm, I realise my own end is fast approaching. My dear Holmes, the last months have been the happiest of my life. I bid you a fond adieu. 'The Choir' is henceforth disbanded.

Yours affectionately,

Wagstaff ...

Acknowledgements

I should like especially to thank Andrea Plunket of the Conan Doyle Literary Trust; my editor Jonathan Ingoldby; Carol Biss, Joanna Bentley, Janet Wrench and all the team at Book Guild Publishing; Amanda Payne for all her hard work; and Olivia Guest at Jonathan Clowes Literary Agents Ltd.